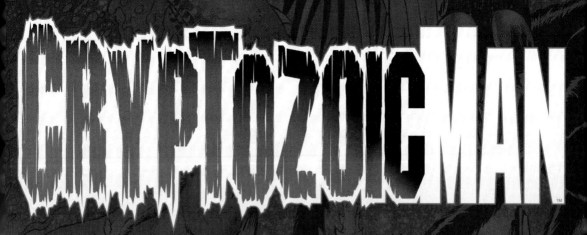

CRYPTOZOICMAN

volume one: DECAPITATION STRIKE

story by
BRYAN JOHNSON and **WALTER FLANAGAN**
written by
BRYAN JOHNSON
pencils by
WALTER FLANAGAN
inks by
CHRIS IVY
colors by
WAYNE JANSEN
letters by
MARSHALL DILLON
cover by
WALTER FLANAGAN and **WAYNE JANSEN**

special thanks to
KEVIN SMITH, MICHAEL ZAPCIC, and MING CHEN

edited by **JOSEPH RYBANDT**
collection design by **JASON ULLMEYER**

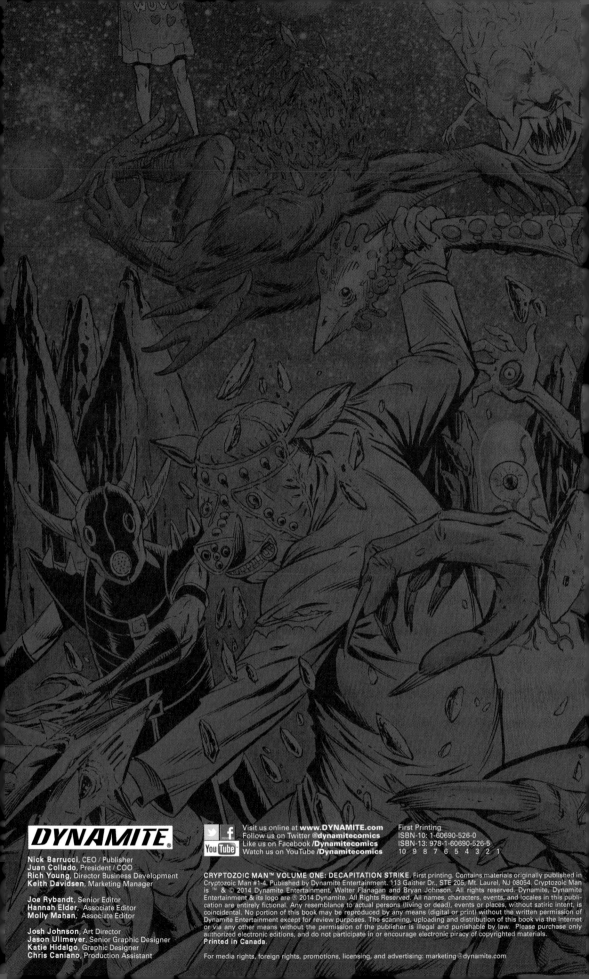

DYNAMITE®

Nick Barrucci, CEO / Publisher
Juan Collado, President / COO
Rich Young, Director Business Development
Keith Davidsen, Marketing Manager

Joe Rybandt, Senior Editor
Hannah Elder, Associate Editor
Molly Mahan, Associate Editor

Josh Johnson, Art Director
Jason Ullmeyer, Senior Graphic Designer
Katie Hidalgo, Graphic Designer
Chris Caniano, Production Assistant

Visit us online at **www.DYNAMITE.com**
Follow us on Twitter **@dynamitecomics**
Like us on Facebook **/Dynamitecomics**
Watch us on YouTube **/Dynamitecomics**

First Printing
ISBN-10: 1-60690-526-0
ISBN-13: 978-1-60690-526-5
10 9 8 7 6 5 4 3 2 1

INTRODUCTION BY BRIAN QUINN

OF *IMPRACTICAL JOKERS*

I've been working with Bryan Johnson and Walt Flanagan for a long time now. Aside from a friendship that is approaching 20 years (!!!!!!), I've been lucky enough to host the award winning (in 2012, at least) podcast Tell Em' Steve-Dave with them since 2010.

I've been pretty fortunate to find myself in the company of such insanely funny, unique individuals. Did I say unique? I mean "fucked up." But in the best way possible. I mean, Walt has declared himself the "only sane man on the planet" and he believes it. He also believes that San Francisco is the worst place in America, and that we'd all be better off if it slid into the ocean.

Some other beliefs of Walt Flanagan -

- Alcohol should be abolished. Or at least mixed with human feces so that the only way to get drunk would be to eat human waste. This, he believes, will stop people from drinking.
- The best way to prolong ejaculation during sex is to think about Spider-Man.
- You can tell friendly aliens apart from evil aliens by if they're wearing shorts when they abduct you.
- Time travel is real, and you're stupid if you don't believe it.
- Applebee's is a hot romantic date spot.
- Kids today should be banned from owning any and all "gizmos" or "gadgets."
- Another man named "Sunday Jeff" is his soul mate.

He's never given a concrete reason for either of these beliefs, but that matters naught to him. Nor should it matter to us. It's best if we just let Walt be Walt and bask in his brilliance.

Listeners of Tell Em Steve-Dave (and why doesn't that include you?) know that even a partial list of reasons that Bryan Johnson is "unique" would take far more room than I'm allotted here. I wouldn't know where to start. The hand gun in the bedroom? The boyhood fishing trips with a strange man wearing testicle revealing short shorts? The brief, but eventful friendship with a drug addicted go-go dancer? The fist fights with his father over a pet scorpion? The time his girlfriend went to the corner store and Bryan slept with her mother?

Bryan Johnson is the guy that Hunter S. Thompson would be if he spent less time writing and more time doing insane shit.

It really is a privilege to be able to hang out with these guys week in and week out and have fun and be creative.

I was supposed to write Cryptozoic Man with these guys. That was the original plan. We had spent some time kicking around ideas that would allow for Walt to draw really nightmarish and bizarre visuals. We were going to write it and self publish it and sell it ourselves. Mainly to our podcast audience because we never ask them for anything and they come through for us time and time again. Then, when they decided to include the comic as a storyline on Comic Book Men, it no longer made sense for me to be involved, so I stepped back.

I might have been upset at this turn of events. I love comics, and its a dream of mine to write them, so this seemed like my shot at it. Instead, I was happy about it. I was excited about it. Because this meant that I get to experience Cryptozoic Man the very same way that you are about to - as a reader. I got to sit back and do zero work and just soak in whatever Bryan and Walt turned out together.

Aside from a few early pages, I declined to read or see any of the work that the guys did until it was published. I wanted to come to the book unspoiled.

This was risky. It was risky because nobody bats a thousand. Nobody. And when a couple of your boys hand you something that they worked so hard on for months and months, you want to like it.

It's no guarantee that you will. You may be left standing there with a steaming turd in your hands, looking at two of your best friends struggling to come up with something to say besides "homina homina homina" and that, dear reader, is not a situation that you want to find yourself in. Then you're stuck with two really bad options.

One, you can lie and say it's great and wince as your friends present to the world something that sucks. This is not something that would work with these guys. Bryan and Walt do not have the sort of ego that demands that sort of soft soaping.

Two, you can shoot straight with your friends and tell them that they better batten down the hatches because the public at large is about to tear them a new hole.

Luckily, no such quandary presented itself to me. I love Cryptozoic Man. It's a beautiful and as weird as the men who created it.

Cryptozoic Man is something special. Walt and Bryan have created something that embodies one of the things that I love most about comics. It presents a story and images that absolutely can not, will not be found anywhere else.

You can do anything in comics and not worry about a budget. In comics, a panel containing the image of a planet exploding costs the same as, say, a leprechaun complaining about his knee pain. Superheroes were flying in comics long before they zoomed across our movie screen. You can do things in comics that you can't do anywhere else. Or, you used to. In this age of great comic book movies and TV shows, it's become common place for images that were once exclusive to comics to become beautifully realized.

This is why Cryptozoic Man is so special. Here, Walt and Bryan bring us ideas that no Hollywood executive is gonna wrap his money hungry head around.

Can you imagine the pitch meeting?

"So, you're saying that Bigfoot is a doorway? How is he a door?"

"This clown, does he crack jokes? How can we make him more likable?"

"What if the little girl just wept regular tears instead of blood? Our focus tests have shown that audiences like it better when little kids don't bleed. Better yet, what about happy tears?"

"This pile of dead aliens, what if they were alive? And what if they befriended the little girl and helped her fight against some neighborhood bullies?"

"What if instead of being made up of a bunch of different monster parts, Cryptozoic Man was made up of, say, Bruce Willis?"

"What does Cryptozoic mean anyway? It'll never play in middle America. How about we call him Monster Dude?"

At this point, the soulless executives would start drooling at the prospect of Bruce Willis playing Monster Dude and spawning a new franchise of movies, followed by an animated series and merchandise galore.

(I'm actually kind of intrigued by this idea. I'd go see a Bruce Willis movie entitled Monster Dude. Shit, I think I'm part of the problem.)

My point it, I feel safe saying that there will never be a movie based on Cryptozoic Man. It's too weird. It's too out there. It's too violent. It's too ORIGINAL. It's something that could only be done in comics, and I'm so glad that Bryan and Walt made it. I'm so glad that Dynamite had the balls to produce it. I'm so glad that I had nothing to do with it, because I get to read it over and over again and pick up something new every time I do.

This is where I'll leave you, my friends. I know you didn't buy this book for the intro from a basic cable z-lister. You bought it for the same reason I'm going to buy it, because you want to bask in the joy of a comic book done right. You want to see something that you will not see anywhere else, even if it's a bit disturbing. Or, you bought it because Walt made it part of a Booty Time Deal, and who can resist those?

– Brian Quinn

P.S. I lied about me buying this book. Without a doubt I'm just going to snag one off the shelf the next time I'm down in Red Bank hanging out with the guys. This is also how I got my Clerks 2 blu ray disc.

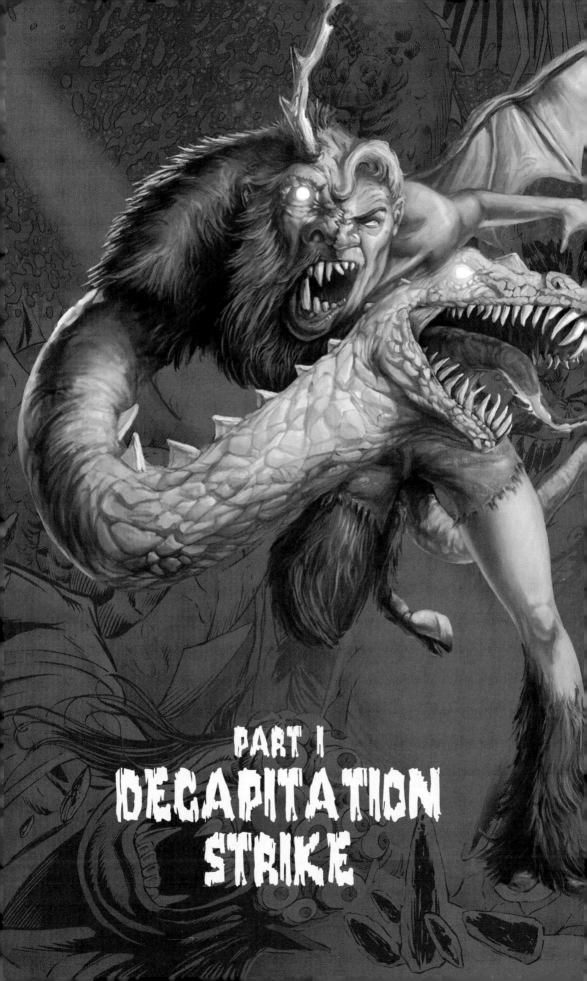

PART 1
DECAPITATION STRIKE

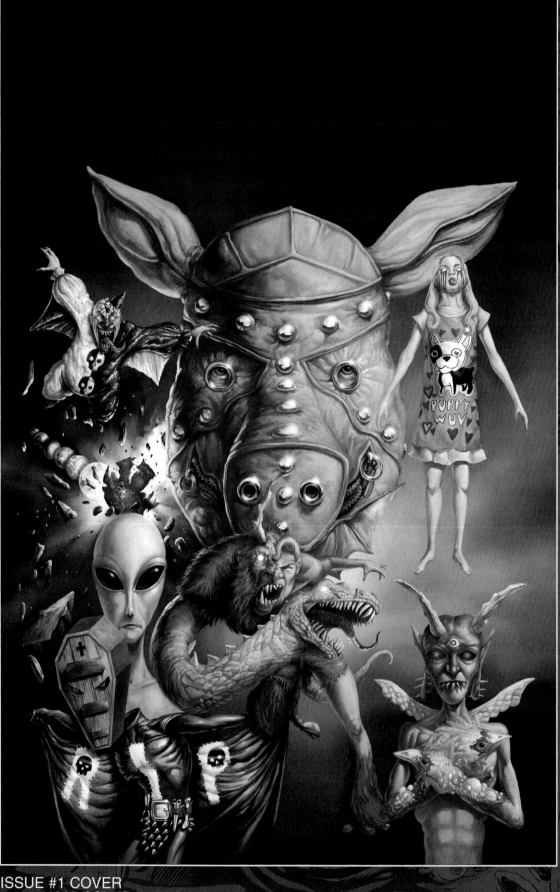

ISSUE #1 COVER
art by **WALTER FLANAGAN** colors by **WAYNE JANSEN**

"THESE HUNGRY GHOSTS WHO WALK AMONGST US. THEIR WAKING LIVES LONG ATROPHIED... THEIR PROMISE ABANDONED...
"...CONTENT TO SUFFER FRAGMENTED TRUTHS UNTIL OBLIVION, AND ALONG WITH IT, THE DREAM'S END.
"MRS. HAMMOND WAS SCOLDING BRANTFORD FOR ROUTING ABOUT IN HER TULIP BED. HER EYES WEREN'T WHAT THEY ONCE WERE...
...OR SHE'D HAVE NOTICED THE SUDDEN CRIMSON RIM OF THE HORIZON.
"EDDIE 'BUG-TURD.' A NEWSPAPER 'BOY' WHO HAD THREE DRUG INDUCED STROKES BY THE TIME HE TURNED THIRTY-ONE WAS RUNNING BEHIND ON DELIVERIES.
"IF ANYONE CARED ENOUGH TO ASK HIM WHY, HE'D HAVE TOLD THEM HIS MOM 'MESSED WITH HIS SNEAKERS.'
"THIN VENEER OF PRETENSE LENDS READILY TO DELUSION. IN THE RIPPLING CURRENTS OF THE RUEFUL STREAM, REGARD EXISTS...
"...THAT SOMEHOW, AN ADULTERESS WOULD BE FAVORED ABOVE THE FLOTSAM OF HUMANITY."
PRIDE.
GLUTTONY.
LUST.
"JOHN OF PATMOS WAS RIGHT. THE SUN BECAME BLACK AS SACKCLOTH AND THE VIALS OF WRATH WERE POURED UPON THE EARTH.
"...BUT IT HAD NOTHING TO DO WITH THE LORD."

Now commandeth all men everywhere to REPENT
ISAIAH 41-10
Let us therefore come boldly to the throne of grace, that we may obtain mercy and find grace to help in time of need

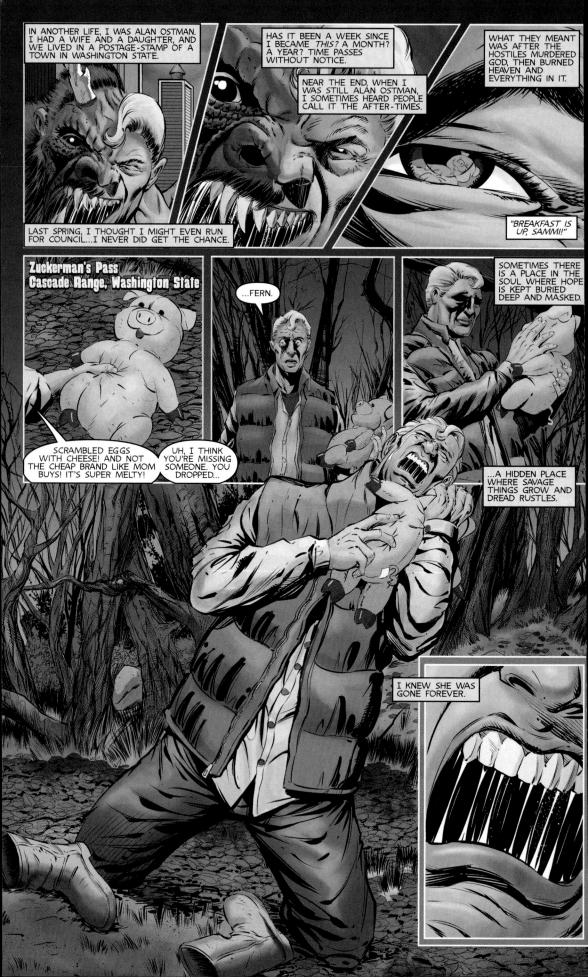

IN ANOTHER LIFE, I WAS ALAN OSTMAN. I HAD A WIFE AND A DAUGHTER, AND WE LIVED IN A POSTAGE-STAMP OF A TOWN IN WASHINGTON STATE.

HAS IT BEEN A WEEK SINCE I BECAME *THIS?* A MONTH? A YEAR? TIME PASSES WITHOUT NOTICE.

NEAR THE END, WHEN I WAS STILL ALAN OSTMAN, I SOMETIMES HEARD PEOPLE CALL IT THE AFTER-TIMES.

WHAT THEY MEANT WAS AFTER THE HOSTILES MURDERED GOD, THEN BURNED HEAVEN AND EVERYTHING IN IT.

"BREAKFAST IS UP, SAMMI!"

LAST SPRING, I THOUGHT I MIGHT EVEN RUN FOR COUNCIL...I NEVER DID GET THE CHANCE.

Zuckerman's Pass
Cascade Range, Washington State

SCRAMBLED EGGS WITH CHEESE! AND NOT THE CHEAP BRAND LIKE MOM BUYS! IT'S SUPER MELTY!

...FERN.

UH, I THINK YOU'RE MISSING SOMEONE. YOU DROPPED...

SOMETIMES THERE IS A PLACE IN THE SOUL WHERE HOPE IS KEPT BURIED DEEP AND MASKED.

...A HIDDEN PLACE WHERE SAVAGE THINGS GROW AND DREAD RUSTLES.

I KNEW SHE WAS GONE FOREVER.

I WAS HER FATHER...
HER PROTECTOR...
I FAILED HER AND SHE PAID WITH HER LIFE. AS DID I.
YOU DIE NEXT, PIG MAN!

IS THAT WHAT YOU BELIEVE, *MONNNN-STER?*
WHY DO YOU *MAINNNN-TAIN* LOYALTY TO THE ARCHITECTS OF YOUR *MALIGNANNN-T* EXISTENCE?
WHAT WAS PROMISED TO YOU TO DESTROY ME AND THEIR PORTALS?
THAT ***YOU*** WOULD BECOME A SAVIOR?
A GOD AMONGST THE WEAKENED MASSES? HE WHO WOULD LEAD MANKIND TO SALVATION THROUGH VALLEYS OF DARKNESS AND THE PROFANE?
WAS THE RETURN OF YOUR SOUL THE BAIT THEY USED, *MONNN-STER?*
...OR SHALL I ASSUME IT WAS LOST FOREVER, ALONG WITH ALL THAT WAS PRECIOUS TO YOU?

BY THEIR HAND, I ENTERED THE FLESH. RESURRECTED. THIS TIME, I AM CHANGED. CARVED NOT IN THE IMAGE OF MAN, BUT OF ANGELS. ANGELS...
...AND TORMENT.
I WAS FILLED WITH THE ROILING WINDS OF TIME AND WAS SORROWFUL, BECAUSE WITH UNMITIGATED CLARITY...
...I KNEW THAT THE FUTILITY OF GOD'S ENDEAVOR WAS ABSOLUTE.
I *AM* THE KNOWLEDGE OF THE AGES. I *AM* THE DESIGN OF CONTRARY. I *AM* VENGEANCE.
IT'S BEEN SAID, JESUS WEPT.
I WILL NOT.

HAVE YOU CONNN-SIDERED YOUR MAKER MAY HAVE ERASED THE PAINNN-FUL MEMORIES CARRIED FROM YOUR HUMA-NNN FORM?
SHED YOUR ANGUISH?
WHAT KIND OF FATHER BURDENS HIS ONLY SON IN SUCH A WAY?
THEY ARE USING YOUR AGONNN-Y...TO FORGIVE THEIR SINNN-S.
B-B-Q
I'M TELLING YOU, WILBUR, IT AIN'T HIM.
HUSH, HUSH, SWEET CHARLOTTE...

OPIE'S
B-B-Q
...'ISSS HIM. FER SHORE...
HELL-RIDER
YEAH, BUT HE GOT A BEARD AND ALL.
FUCK HIS HAIRY-ASS FACE! I COULDN'T NEVER FORGIT A KISSER LIKE 'DAT. EVEN WIT' HIS SHIT DISGUISE!
TRUS' ME. I SEEN HIS PITCHER' ON THE INNER'NET LOTSA' TIMES.
YOU DIDN'T HAPPEN TO BE USING THE "INNER'NET" AT THE "LIBERRY," DID YOU?
KEEP CRACKIN' WISE, WHY DON'CHA? 'CEPT IT'S ME, NOT YOUR KID YOU UP AGAINST 'AN...
...MAYBE IT'S *YOU* THEY WON' BE FINDIN' HIDE NOR HAIR OF...
...THIS TIME.
HUH?!
OSTMAN.
I IMAGINE LITTLE SAMMI...

...MUST SMELL ALMOST AS BAD AS YOU DO BY NOW.
YOU... DON'T...SAY... HER...
...NAME!
DOWN, BOY!
BAD DOG!
EEEEE HAAAAA!!
AHHHHHHH!!!

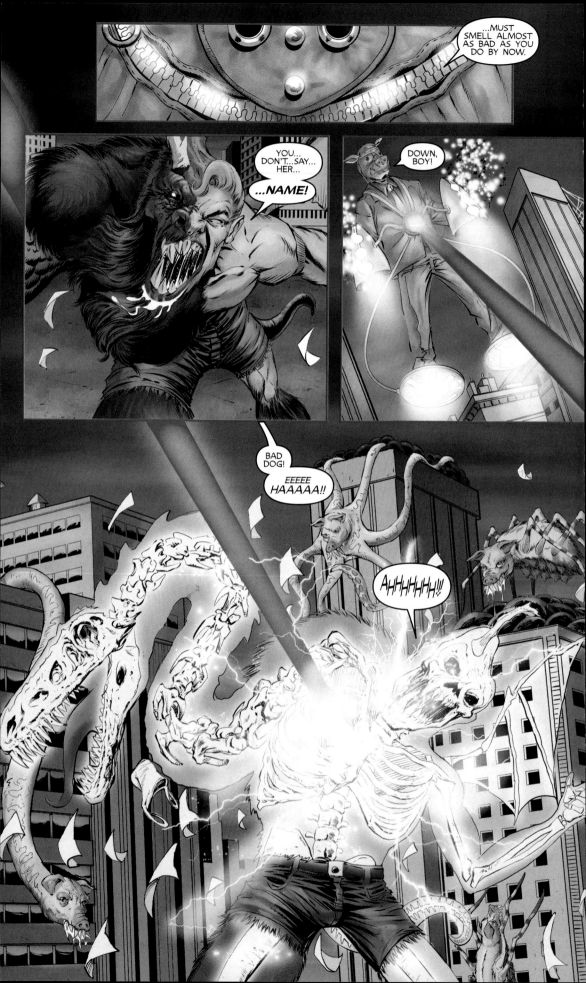

EEEEYAHHH!!!
OSTMAN.
OPIE'S
B-B-Q
HOW...

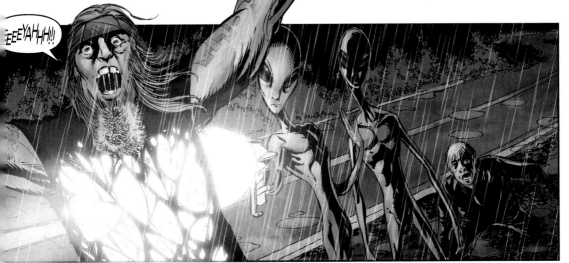

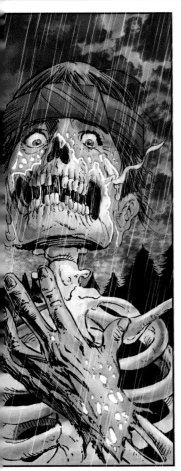

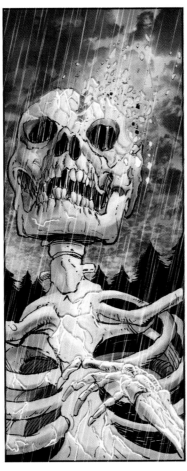

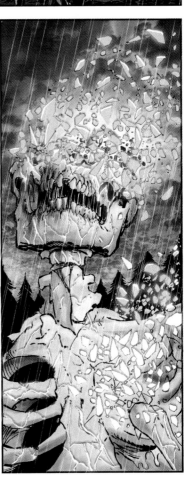

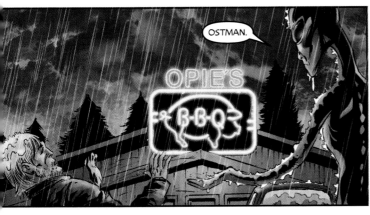

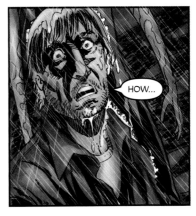

LOOK WITHIN.
IT'S WITHIN.

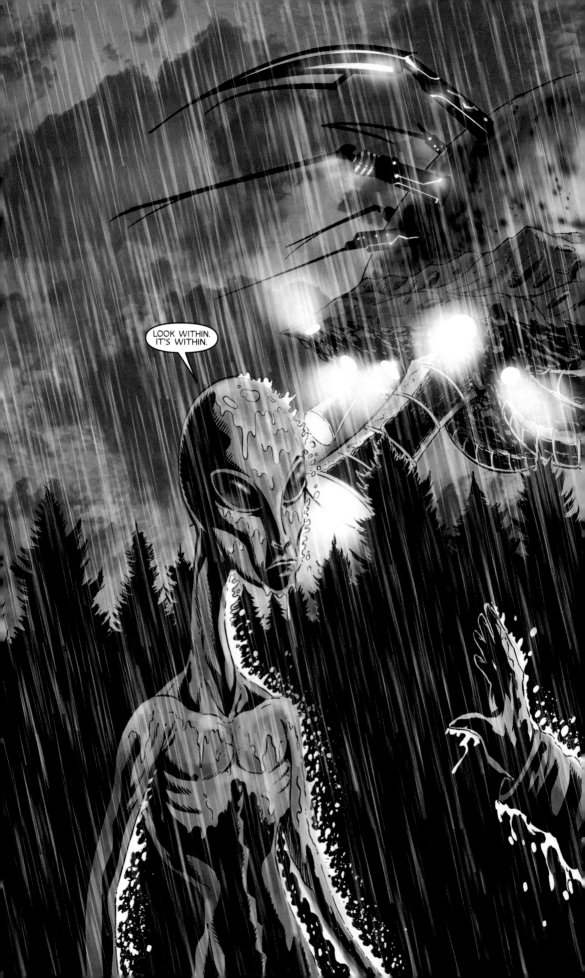

WITHIN YOU, OSTMAN.

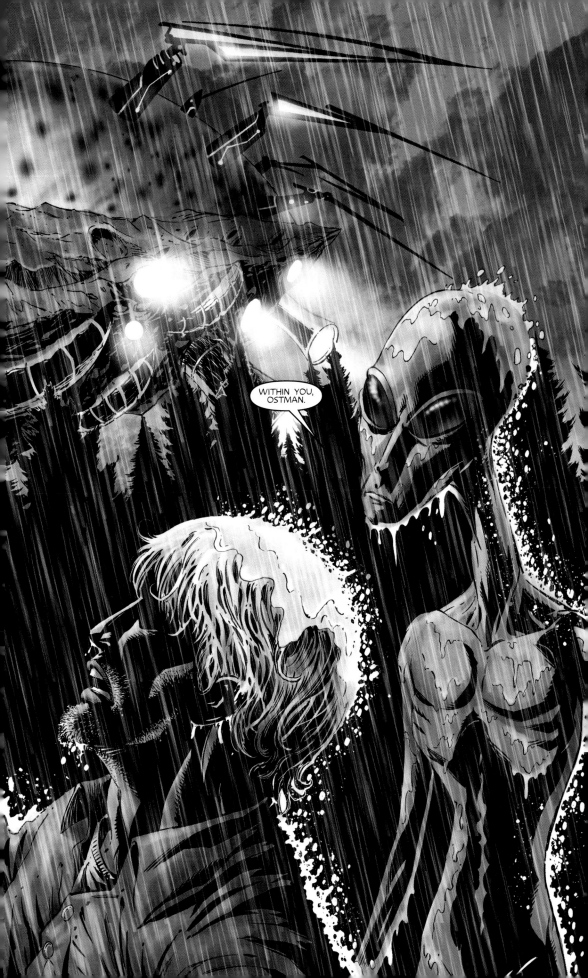

DADDY? I CAN'T SEE YOU.
DADDY? I CAN'T SEE YOU.
DADDY? I CAN'T SEE YOU.
DADDY? I CAN'T SEE YOU.
DADDY? I CAN'T SEE YOU.
DADDY? I CAN'T SEE YOU.
DADDY? I CAN'T SEE YOU.
DADDY? I CAN'T SEE YOU.
DADDY? I CAN'T SEE YOU.
DADDY? I CAN'T SEE YOU.
DADDY? I CAN'T SEE YOU.
DADDY? I CAN'T SEE YOU.
DADDY? I CAN'T SEE YOU.
DADDY? I CAN'T SEE YOU.
DADDY? I CAN'T SEE YOU.
DADDY? I CAN'T SEE YOU.
DADDY? I CAN'T SEE YOU.
DADDY? I CAN'T SEE YOU.
DADDY? I CAN'T SEE YOU.
DADDY? I CAN'T SEE YOU.

I ONCE KNEW A *WOMA-NNN*, A LOVELY *PERSO-NNN* BY *ANNN-YONE'S STANNN-DARDS*.
HOW SHE LOVED TO BE *PUNNN-ISHED!*
OOOOOO... THE *NNN-OISES* SHE WOULD MAKE, LET ME TELL YOU! LIKE AN *ANNN-IMAL*.
...AND ALL I GOT FROM HE OLD MAN'S SIDE OF THE FAMILY WAS A RECEDING *HAIRLINNN-E*.
HAHAHA HAHAHA HAHA!!!
DADDY? I CAN'T FIND FERN. HAVE YOU SEEN HER?
SAMMI?

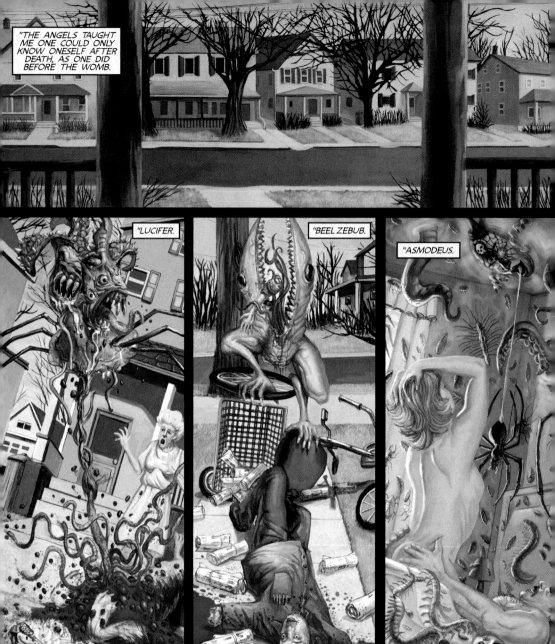

"THE ANGELS TAUGHT ME ONE COULD ONLY KNOW ONESELF AFTER DEATH, AS ONE DID BEFORE THE WOMB.

"LUCIFER.

"BEEL ZEBUB.

"ASMODEUS.

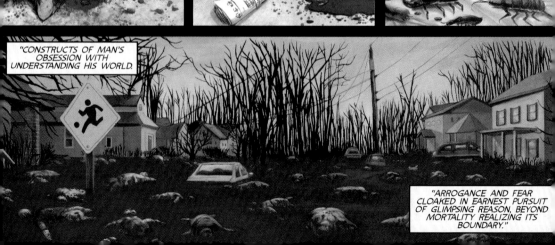

"CONSTRUCTS OF MAN'S OBSESSION WITH UNDERSTANDING HIS WORLD.

"ARROGANCE AND FEAR CLOAKED IN EARNEST PURSUIT OF GLIMPSING REASON, BEYOND MORTALITY REALIZING ITS BOUNDARY."

SAY IT AI-NNN'T SO! IS THE FUNNN OVER ALREADY?
SAMMI... HOW COULD YOU KNOW? UNLESS...
UNNN-LESS... YES, LOOK AT ME, MONNN-STER!
UNNN-LESS... SAY IT!
YOU CA-NNNN'T BELIEVE IT TO BE TRUE?
CANNN YOU?

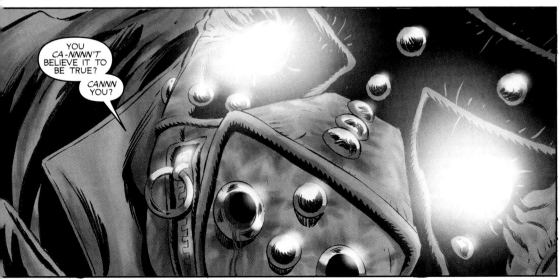

WHEREVER LIGHT SEEKS REFUGE...
...DARKNESS SHALL SURELY PURSUE.
FOOLS AND DREAMERS PROFESS THAT FAITH DEFEATS THE ECLIPSE OF THEIR *HUMANNN*-ITY...

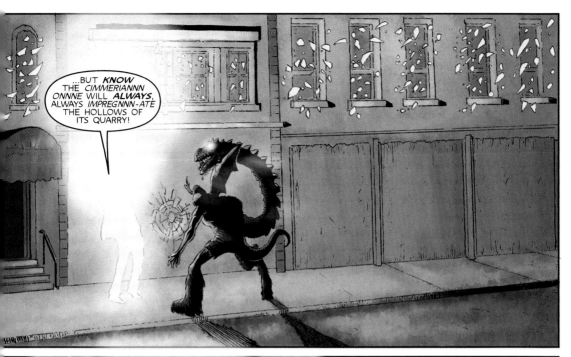

...BUT *KNOW* THE *CIMMERIANNN ONNNE* WILL *ALWAYS*, ALWAYS IMPREGNNN-ATE THE HOLLOWS OF ITS QUARRY!

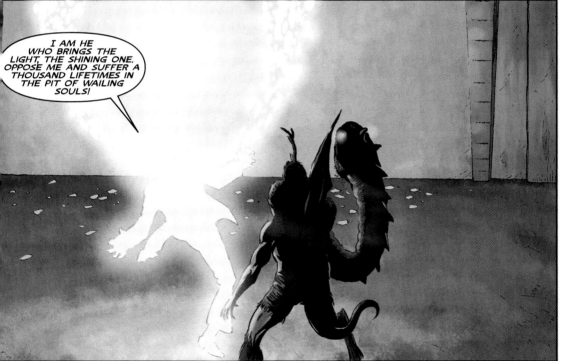

I AM HE WHO BRINGS THE LIGHT, THE SHINING ONE. OPPOSE ME AND SUFFER A THOUSAND LIFETIMES IN THE PIT OF WAILING SOULS!

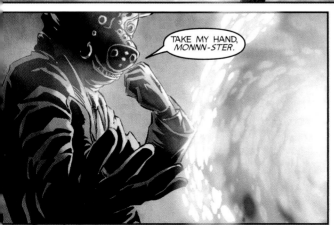

TAKE MY HAND, MONNN-STER.

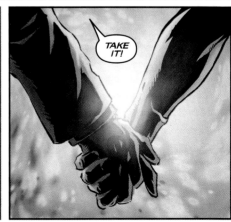

TAKE IT!

...YOUR LITTLE GIRL WAITS.

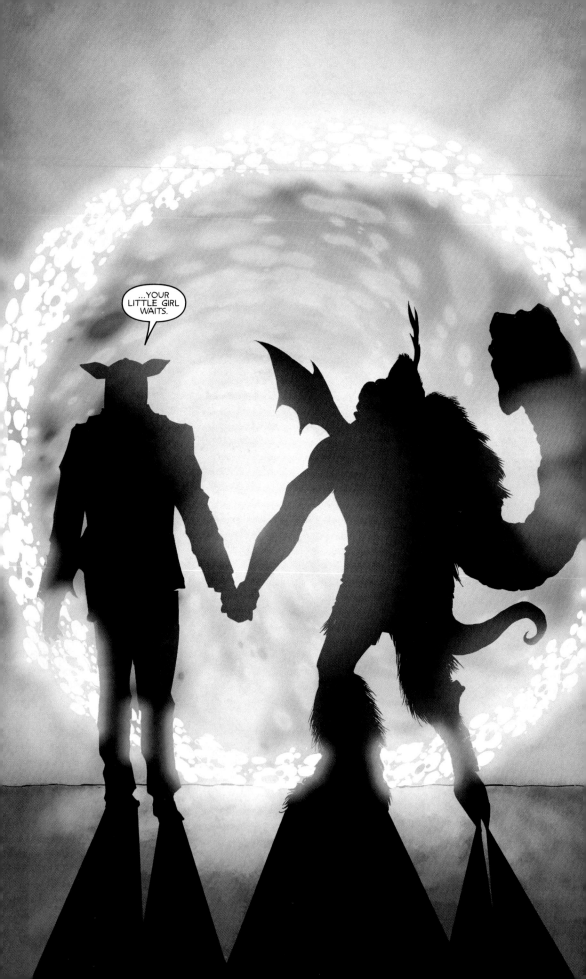

PART II
PLANET KILLER

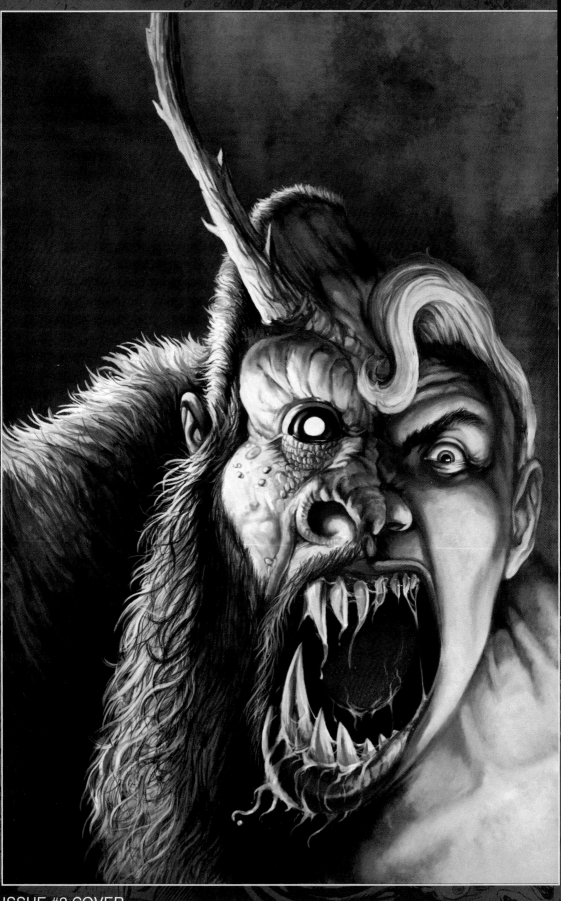

ISSUE #2 COVER
art by **WALTER FLANAGAN** colors by **WAYNE JANSEN**

"THIS LITTLE LIGHT OF MINE...
"I'M GONNA LET IT SHINE.
"LET IT SHINE.
"LET IT SHINE.
"LET IT...

"SHINE."

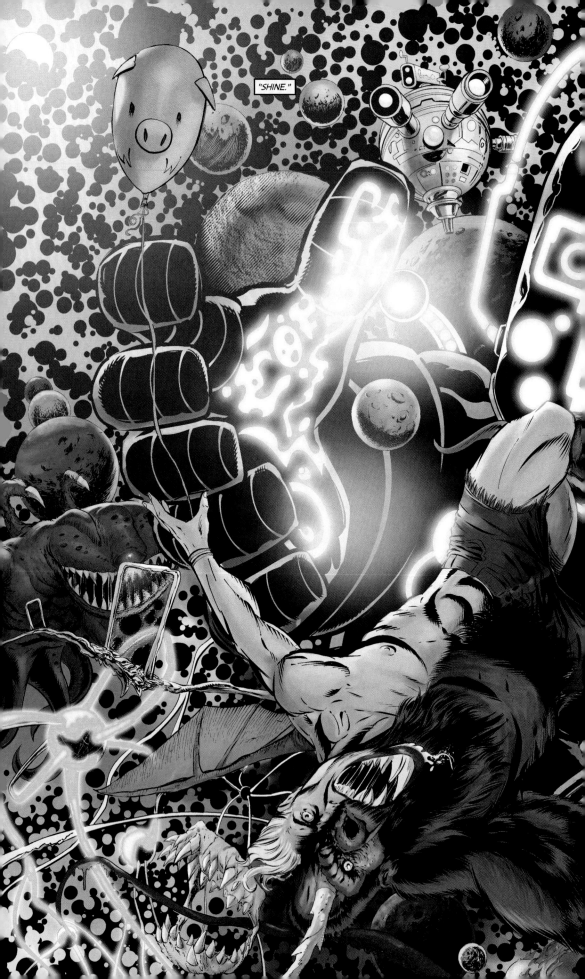

HERE COMES THAT PRIZE PONY OF YOURS, MR. THEAD.
DELIVERED UP AS PROMISED BY YOURS TRULY, FIVE BY FIVE.
YOU KNOW ME, MR. THEAD, I DON'T WANNA NEVER QUESTION YOUR SAVVY.
BUT WE BOTH KNOW...
THE KINDA SHIT SMELLIN' FOUL WE TALKIN' DON'T 'BOUT WASH OFFA NO MAN, MUCH LESS ONE SUCHA' YOUR ALAN OSTMAN.
WHAT IS...THIS PLACE?
"MR. OSTMAN? MR. THEAD WILL SEE YOU NOW."
THE
INDUSTR
MR. OSTMAN?
HUH? OH, I'M SORRY. THANK YOU.
AIN'T EXACTLY THE FROSTY TYPE, IS HE?
cam4 2013.07.09
●REC 10:02.55
THE MOST DANGEROUS TYPE OF MAN IS ONE WHO ALREADY DONE LOST ALL THAT WAS PRECIOUS TO HIM.

MR. OSTMAN!
AT LONG LAST!
HOLY...
PLEASE, PLEASE...COME IN. I HOPE YOU WEREN'T WAITING TOO LONG.
I MUST SAY, THIS IS A PLEASURE FAR TOO LONG IN THE MAKING.
SORRY. I THINK MY HAND IS STILL CRAMPED FROM SIGNING ALL THE CONFIDENTIALITY AGREEMENTS.
THE ONLY TIME I CANNOT BEAR SECRECY IS WHEN IT IS USED AS A WEAPON TO PROLONG IGNORANCE.
OTHERWISE, YOU JUST A BIG OL' PAIR'A LOOSE LIP AIN'TCHA, MR. OSTMAN?

THIS, YOUR WORK, MY GOD, MAN... IT'S HIGH ART.
THE MOMENT I FINISHED READING IT, I SAID...BRING ME ALAN OSTMAN.
I CONFESS TO FINDING YOUR THEORIES ON DIMENSION NETWORKS ESPECIALLY INTERESTING.
WELL, THANK YOU, BUT CAN WE BACK UP A FEW STEPS?
I'M NOT SURE WHY I'M HERE. OR HOW YOU KNEW WHERE TO FIND ME, CONSIDERING...
BAIL? WHO?
DON'T HE KNOW ALL ABOUT YOU, BOY? OL' MR. METRIS THEAD BEEN STUDYING YOU UP, DOWN, AND SIDEWAYS FOR SOME TIME.
HE KNOW YOUR LITTLE ONE DISAPPEAR THAT DAY AND EVER'BODY BLAME YOU. PAPERS EVEN SAY MAYBE YOU UP AND KILT YOUR OWN GIRL.
...AN YOUR WIFE LEAVIN' HER BLOODY CARCASS FOR YOU TO FIND AFTER DOIN' HERSELF IN? IN'NT THAT JUST PURE TYPE HATE?
ALAN OSTMAN

I'VE READ JUST ABOUT ANYTHING YOU'VE WRITTEN, MR. OSTMAN. THOUGH DIFFICULT TO TRACK DOWN, YOUR MASTER'S THESIS "OF GODS AND CRYPTIDS" WAS AN ILLUMINATING READ.
I'M FLATTERED, BUT...
THAT PAPER...
...IS WHY YOU'RE HERE.
...AND WHY I'D LIKE YOU TO WORK FOR ME.
MR. THEAD, I HAVE NO IDEA WHAT IT IS YOU **DO** HERE OR WHAT...
OF COURSE YOU DON'T. IT'S A SENSITIVE PROJECT, MR. OSTMAN. ONE I FEEL ONLY YOU ARE SUITED FOR. COME WITH ME, I'D LIKE TO SHOW YOU SOMETHING.
I'M NOT A JUDGMENTAL MAN...
...YOUR AFOREMENTIONED LEGAL ISSUES...
...ARE OF LITTLE CONCERN TO ME.
WANNA GO BACK TO SHAKIN' LIKE A LEAF WHILE YA POCKET A FUN-SIZE CANDY BAR AT THE TILLAMOOK FIVE AND DIME? MANNERS, BOY!
I APPRECIATE THAT. TRUST HAS BEEN A RARE COMMODITY IN MY LIFE THIS PAST YEAR.

HOT DAMN! NOW THIS IS A SIGHT! AIN'T THIS A SIGHT, OSTMAN? MR. THEAD BUILT HISSELF AN ALIEN IN THIS VERY LAB.
MY GOD. WHAT IS THIS PLACE?
PENDING A MUTUALLY AGREEABLE ARRANGEMENT, IT'S YOUR NEW LAB.

I'VE NEVER SEEN ANYTHING LIKE IT.
'COURSE YA HAVEN'T, FOOL!
WORLD'S MOST ADVANCED GOVERNMENTS WOULD BE SLOBBERIN' WHAT MR. THEAD HAVE HERE.
I NEED TO ASK...
...WHY ME?
I FIND US TO BE KINDRED SOULS INASMUCH AS YOU AREN'T AFRAID TO PUSH THE BOUNDARIES OF THE SCIENCE WE PRACTICE.
YOU ARE ONE OF THE FEW ALLIES OUR COMMUNITY HAS. ONE UNAFRAID TO EXIST OUTSIDE THE REALM WHERE OPINION IS OF CONSEQUENCE.
I'M PRETTY SURE THAT'S THE MOST COLORFUL WAY I'VE EVER BEEN CALLED A QUACK.
IN A WORLD OF RAMPANT AND UNCHECKED CYNICISM, WE QUACKS HAVE ONLY EACH OTHER TO LEAN ON.
NO. IT CAN'T BE. IS THAT A...
KORRING DISSIMILATING REFRACTOR. ONE OF THE FIVE THAT SAW MANUFACTURE...OF WHICH ONLY TWO SURVIVED THE FALL OF THE THIRD REICH.
WHERE DID YOU...I MEAN, I'VE NEVER ACTUALLY SEEN ONE. I THOUGHT IT WAS DEBUNKED AS AN INTERNET HOAX YEARS AGO.
ISN'T THAT WHAT ***THEY***, THE SNEERING RATIONALISTS, WOULD LOVE TO HAVE US BELIEVE?

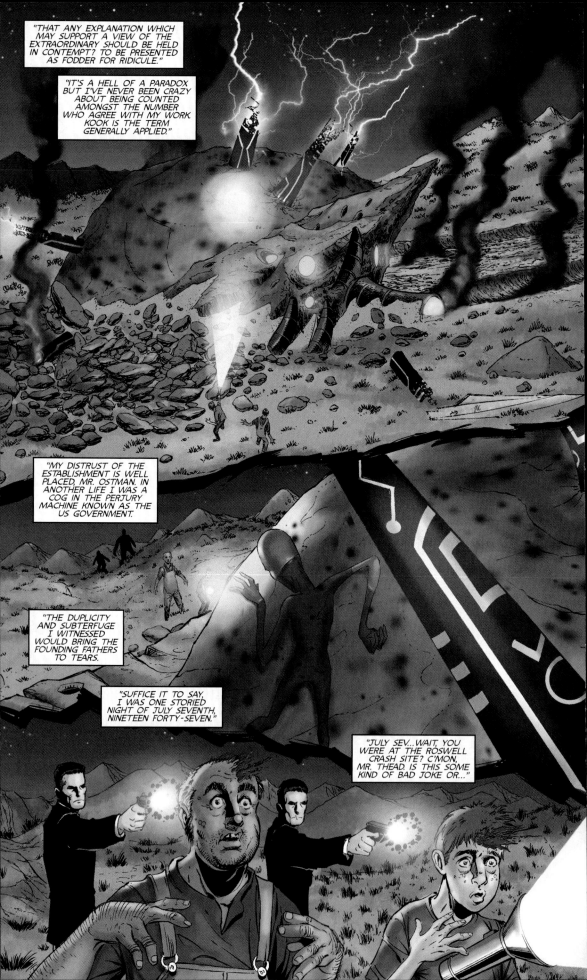

"THAT ANY EXPLANATION WHICH MAY SUPPORT A VIEW OF THE EXTRAORDINARY SHOULD BE HELD IN CONTEMPT? TO BE PRESENTED AS FODDER FOR RIDICULE."

"IT'S A HELL OF A PARADOX BUT I'VE NEVER BEEN CRAZY ABOUT BEING COUNTED AMONGST THE NUMBER WHO AGREE WITH MY WORK. KOOK IS THE TERM GENERALLY APPLIED."

"MY DISTRUST OF THE ESTABLISHMENT IS WELL PLACED, MR. OSTMAN. IN ANOTHER LIFE I WAS A COG IN THE PERJURY MACHINE KNOWN AS THE US GOVERNMENT.

"THE DUPLICITY AND SUBTERFUGE I WITNESSED WOULD BRING THE FOUNDING FATHERS TO TEARS.

"SUFFICE IT TO SAY, I WAS ONE STORIED NIGHT OF JULY SEVENTH, NINETEEN FORTY-SEVEN."

"JULY SEV...WAIT, YOU WERE AT THE ROSWELL CRASH SITE? C'MON, MR. THEAD, IS THIS SOME KIND OF BAD JOKE OR..."

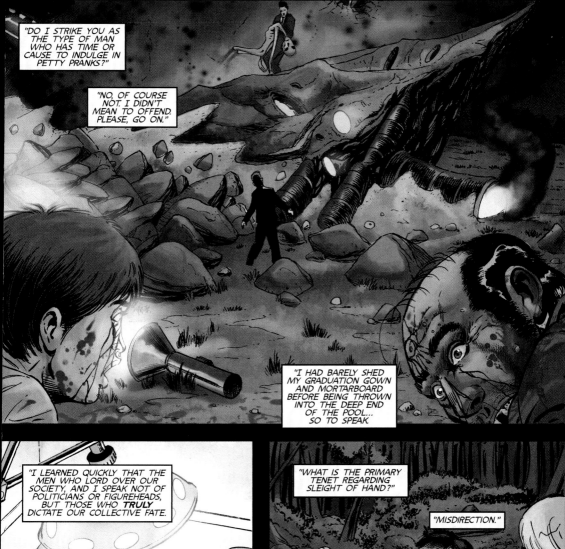

"DO I STRIKE YOU AS THE TYPE OF MAN WHO HAS TIME OR CAUSE TO INDULGE IN PETTY PRANKS?"

"NO, OF COURSE NOT. I DIDN'T MEAN TO OFFEND. PLEASE, GO ON."

"I HAD BARELY SHED MY GRADUATION GOWN AND MORTARBOARD BEFORE BEING THROWN INTO THE DEEP END OF THE POOL... SO TO SPEAK."

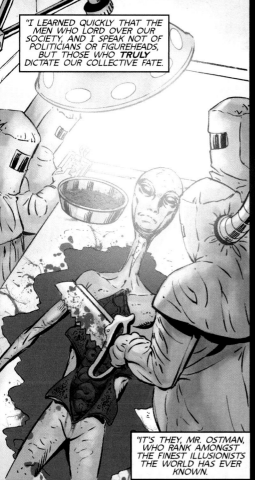

"I LEARNED QUICKLY THAT THE MEN WHO LORD OVER OUR SOCIETY, AND I SPEAK NOT OF POLITICIANS OR FIGUREHEADS, BUT THOSE WHO **TRULY** DICTATE OUR COLLECTIVE FATE.

"IT'S THEY, MR. OSTMAN, WHO RANK AMONGST THE FINEST ILLUSIONISTS THE WORLD HAS EVER KNOWN."

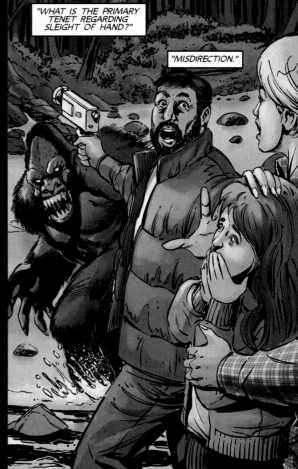

"WHAT IS THE PRIMARY TENET REGARDING SLEIGHT OF HAND?"

"MISDIRECTION."

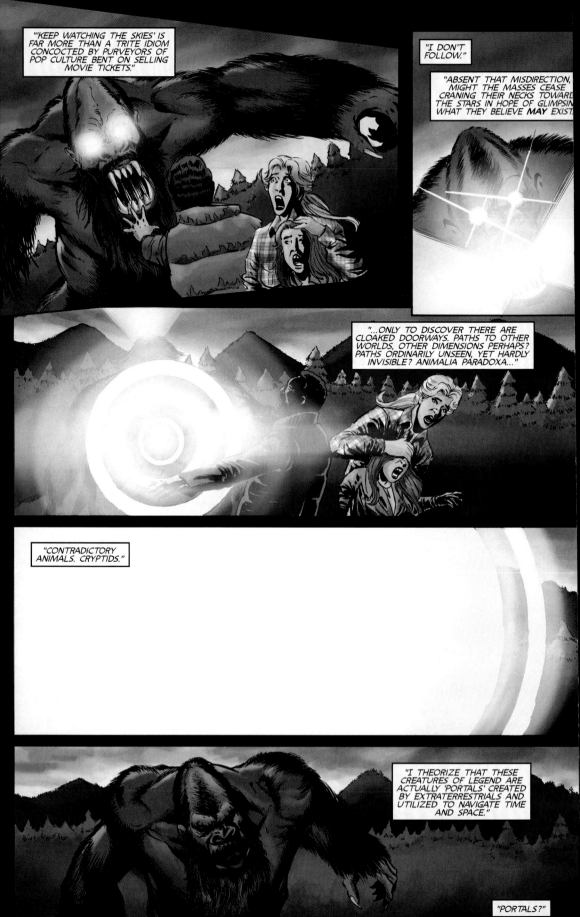

"'KEEP WATCHING THE SKIES' IS FAR MORE THAN A TRITE IDIOM CONCOCTED BY PURVEYORS OF POP CULTURE BENT ON SELLING MOVIE TICKETS."

"I DON'T FOLLOW."

"ABSENT THAT MISDIRECTION, MIGHT THE MASSES CEASE CRANING THEIR NECKS TOWARD THE STARS IN HOPE OF GLIMPSIN WHAT THEY BELIEVE **MAY** EXIST.

"...ONLY TO DISCOVER THERE ARE CLOAKED DOORWAYS. PATHS TO OTHER WORLDS, OTHER DIMENSIONS PERHAPS? PATHS ORDINARILY UNSEEN, YET HARDLY INVISIBLE? ANIMALIA PARADOXA..."

"CONTRADICTORY ANIMALS. CRYPTIDS."

"I THEORIZE THAT THESE CREATURES OF LEGEND ARE ACTUALLY 'PORTALS' CREATED BY EXTRATERRESTRIALS AND UTILIZED TO NAVIGATE TIME AND SPACE."

"PORTALS?"

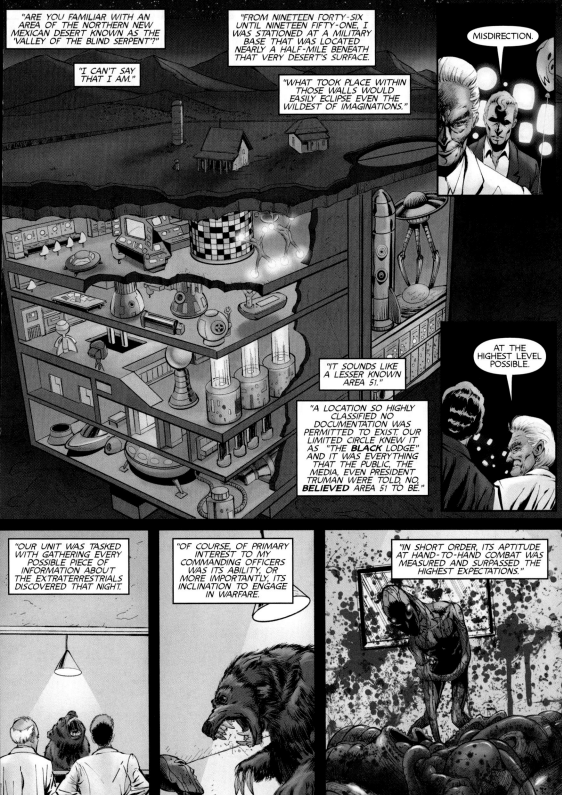

"ARE YOU FAMILIAR WITH AN AREA OF THE NORTHERN NEW MEXICAN DESERT KNOWN AS THE 'VALLEY OF THE BLIND SERPENT'?"

"I CAN'T SAY THAT I AM."

"FROM NINETEEN FORTY-SIX UNTIL NINETEEN FIFTY-ONE, I WAS STATIONED AT A MILITARY BASE THAT WAS LOCATED NEARLY A HALF-MILE BENEATH THAT VERY DESERT'S SURFACE.

"WHAT TOOK PLACE WITHIN THOSE WALLS WOULD EASILY ECLIPSE EVEN THE WILDEST OF IMAGINATIONS."

MISDIRECTION.

"IT SOUNDS LIKE A LESSER KNOWN AREA 51."

"A LOCATION SO HIGHLY CLASSIFIED NO DOCUMENTATION WAS PERMITTED TO EXIST. OUR LIMITED CIRCLE KNEW IT AS "THE **BLACK** LODGE" AND IT WAS EVERYTHING THAT THE PUBLIC, THE MEDIA, EVEN PRESIDENT TRUMAN WERE TOLD, NO, **BELIEVED** AREA 51 TO BE."

AT THE HIGHEST LEVEL POSSIBLE.

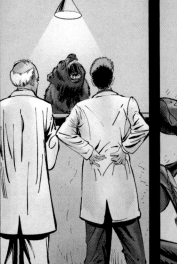

"OUR UNIT WAS TASKED WITH GATHERING EVERY POSSIBLE PIECE OF INFORMATION ABOUT THE EXTRATERRESTRIALS DISCOVERED THAT NIGHT.

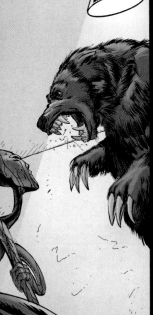

"OF COURSE, OF PRIMARY INTEREST TO MY COMMANDING OFFICERS WAS ITS ABILITY, OR MORE IMPORTANTLY, ITS INCLINATION TO ENGAGE IN WARFARE.

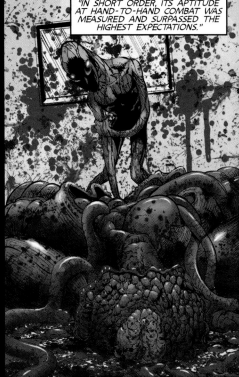

"IN SHORT ORDER, ITS APTITUDE AT HAND-TO-HAND COMBAT WAS MEASURED AND SURPASSED THE HIGHEST EXPECTATIONS."

"MY COLLEAGUES AND I WERE AVERAGE MEN. AVERAGE MEN FROM AVERAGE PLACES. PLACES LIKE WICHITA, KANSAS. BANGOR, MAINE. MULESHOE, TEXAS.
"THE COMMONALITY WHICH BOUND US, ENSURED OUR UNFLATTERING PORTRAYAL AND THE WHOLESALE CONDEMNATION OF MY TEAM'S ETHICAL LEANINGS."
"HOW DO YOU MEAN?"
"MY MEN WERE DISMISSED AS 'DAINTY' AND 'OPERATION APPLE PIE' WAS IMMEDIATELY PUT INTO EFFECT.
"THE 'APPLE PIE' DIRECTORS RECRUITED THE CRUELEST, MOST SINFUL MEMBERS OF THE NAZI TORTURE MACHINE.
"THEY ENLISTED MEN JUDGED TOO DERANGED TO SERVE IN UNIT 731... WELL KNOWN TO BE THE PERSONIFICATION OF FRENZIED SAVAGERY AND BLOODLUST.
CHOLERA
"THESE WERE...
"MEN WITHOUT CONSCIENCE...
"INCAPABLE OF EMPATHY...
"...STRANGERS TO REMORSE."

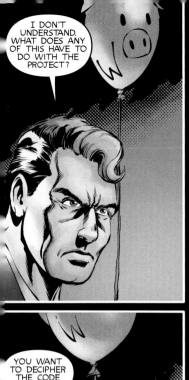

I DON'T UNDERSTAND. WHAT DOES ANY OF THIS HAVE TO DO WITH THE PROJECT?

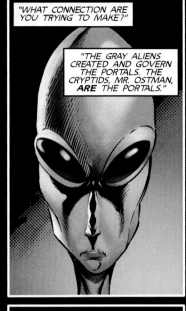

"WHAT CONNECTION ARE YOU TRYING TO MAKE?"

"THE GRAY ALIENS CREATED AND GOVERN THE PORTALS. THE CRYPTIDS, MR. OSTMAN, *ARE THE PORTALS.*"

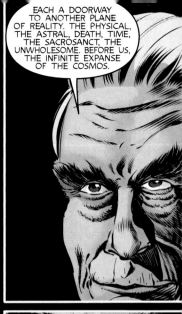

EACH A DOORWAY TO ANOTHER PLANE OF REALITY. THE PHYSICAL, THE ASTRAL, DEATH, TIME, THE SACROSANCT, THE UNWHOLESOME. BEFORE US, THE INFINITE EXPANSE OF THE COSMOS.

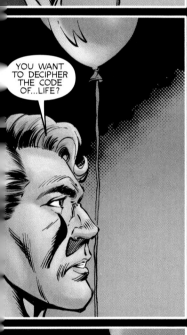

YOU WANT TO DECIPHER THE CODE OF...LIFE?

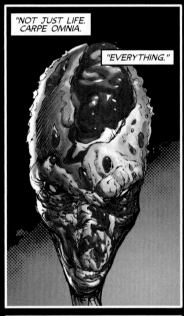

"NOT JUST LIFE. CARPE OMNIA.

"EVERYTHING."

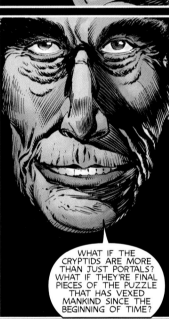

WHAT IF THE CRYPTIDS ARE MORE THAN JUST PORTALS? WHAT IF THEY'RE FINAL PIECES OF THE PUZZLE THAT HAS VEXED MANKIND SINCE THE BEGINNING OF TIME?

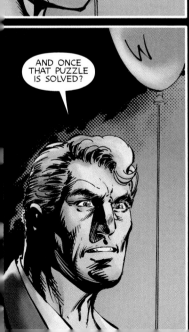

AND ONCE THAT PUZZLE IS SOLVED?

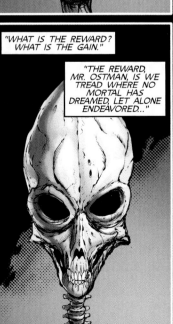

"WHAT IS THE REWARD? WHAT IS THE GAIN."

"THE REWARD, MR. OSTMAN, IS WE TREAD WHERE NO MORTAL HAS DREAMED, LET ALONE ENDEAVORED..."

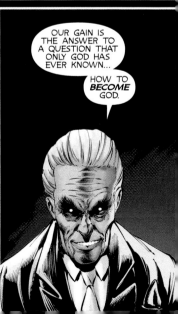

OUR GAIN IS THE ANSWER TO A QUESTION THAT ONLY GOD HAS EVER KNOWN...

HOW TO *BECOME* GOD.

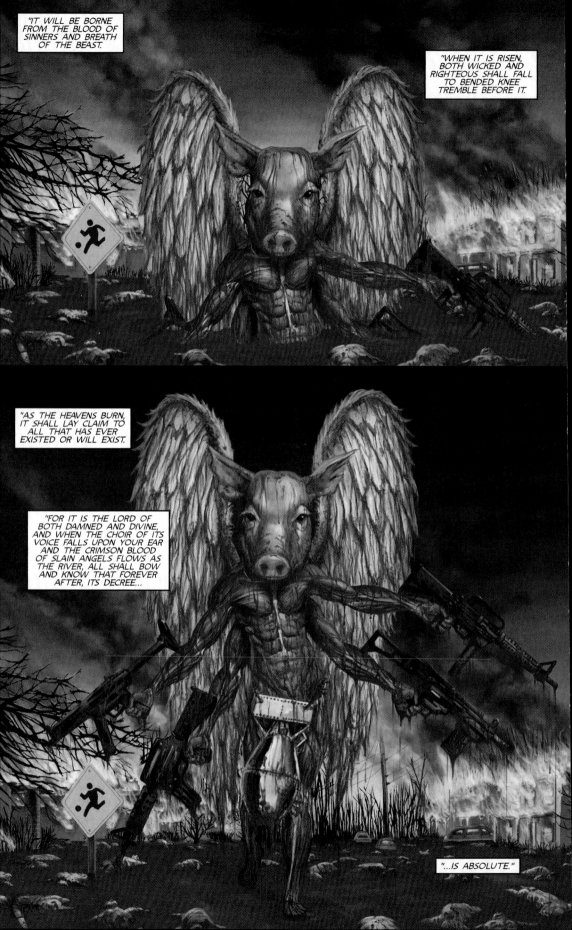

"IT WILL BE BORNE FROM THE BLOOD OF SINNERS AND BREATH OF THE BEAST.

"WHEN IT IS RISEN, BOTH WICKED AND RIGHTEOUS SHALL FALL TO BENDED KNEE TREMBLE BEFORE IT.

"AS THE HEAVENS BURN, IT SHALL LAY CLAIM TO ALL THAT HAS EVER EXISTED OR WILL EXIST.

"FOR IT IS THE LORD OF BOTH DAMNED AND DIVINE, AND WHEN THE CHOIR OF ITS VOICE FALLS UPON YOUR EAR AND THE CRIMSON BLOOD OF SLAIN ANGELS FLOWS AS THE RIVER, ALL SHALL BOW AND KNOW THAT FOREVER AFTER, ITS DECREE...

"...IS ABSOLUTE."

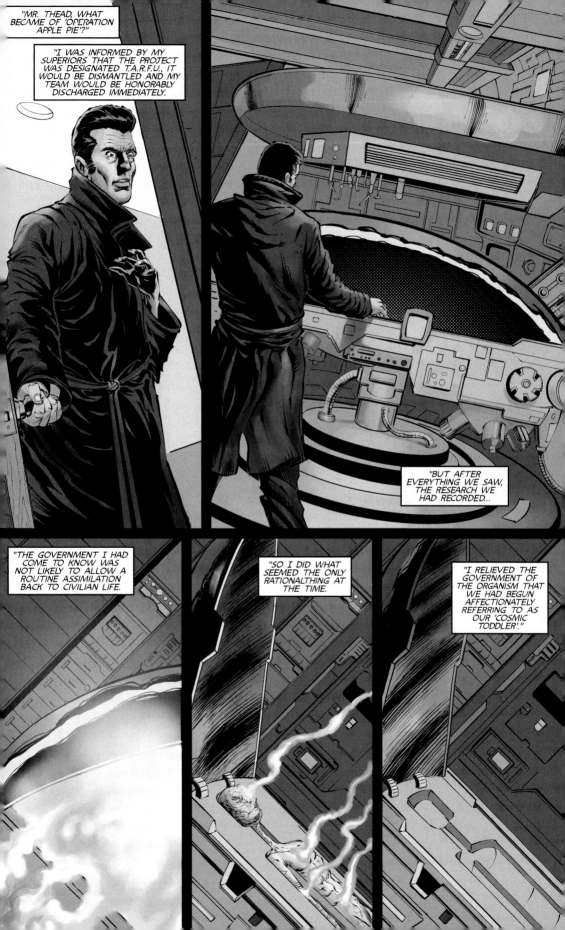

"MR. THEAD, WHAT BECAME OF 'OPERATION APPLE PIE'?"

"I WAS INFORMED BY MY SUPERIORS THAT THE PROJECT WAS DESIGNATED T.A.R.F.U., IT WOULD BE DISMANTLED AND MY TEAM WOULD BE HONORABLY DISCHARGED IMMEDIATELY.

"BUT AFTER EVERYTHING WE SAW, THE RESEARCH WE HAD RECORDED...

"THE GOVERNMENT I HAD COME TO KNOW WAS NOT LIKELY TO ALLOW A ROUTINE ASSIMILATION BACK TO CIVILIAN LIFE.

"SO I DID WHAT SEEMED THE ONLY RATIONAL THING AT THE TIME.

"I RELIEVED THE GOVERNMENT OF THE ORGANISM THAT WE HAD BEGUN AFFECTIONATELY REFERRING TO AS OUR 'COSMIC TODDLER'."

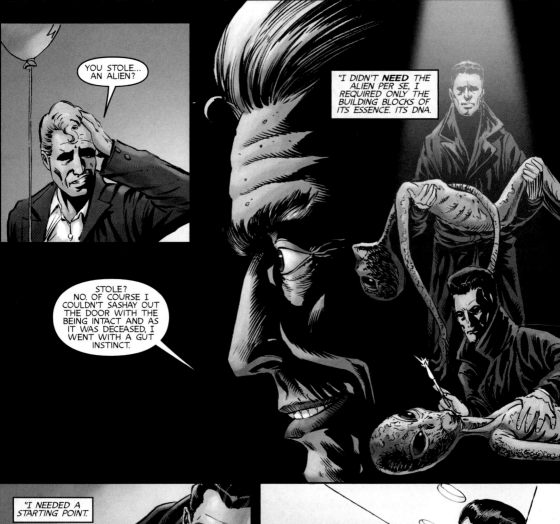

YOU STOLE...
AN ALIEN?

"I DIDN'T **NEED** THE ALIEN PER SE, I REQUIRED ONLY THE BUILDING BLOCKS OF ITS ESSENCE. ITS DNA.

STOLE? NO. OF COURSE I COULDN'T SASHAY OUT THE DOOR WITH THE BEING INTACT AND AS IT WAS DECEASED, I WENT WITH A GUT INSTINCT.

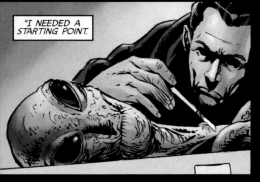

"I NEEDED A STARTING POINT.

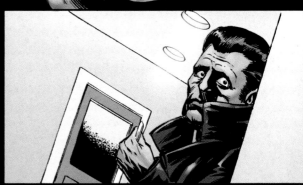

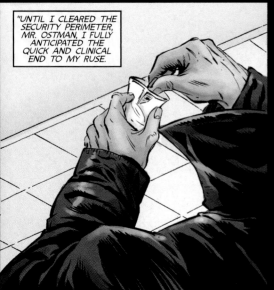

"UNTIL I CLEARED THE SECURITY PERIMETER, MR. OSTMAN, I FULLY ANTICIPATED THE QUICK AND CLINICAL END TO MY RUSE.

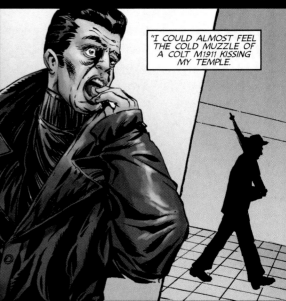

"I COULD ALMOST FEEL THE COLD MUZZLE OF A COLT M1911 KISSING MY TEMPLE.

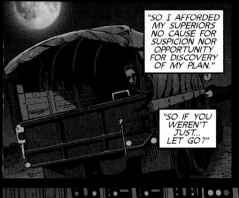

"SO I AFFORDED MY SUPERIORS NO CAUSE FOR SUSPICION NOR OPPORTUNITY FOR DISCOVERY OF MY PLAN."

"SO IF YOU WEREN'T JUST... LET GO?"

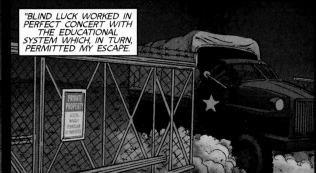

"BLIND LUCK WORKED IN PERFECT CONCERT WITH THE EDUCATIONAL SYSTEM WHICH, IN TURN, PERMITTED MY ESCAPE.

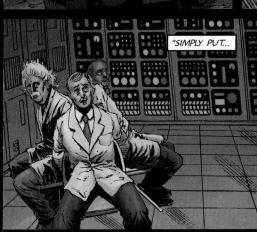

"SIMPLY PUT...

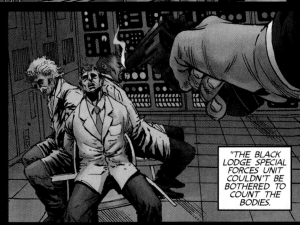

"THE BLACK LODGE SPECIAL FORCES UNIT COULDN'T BE BOTHERED TO COUNT THE BODIES.

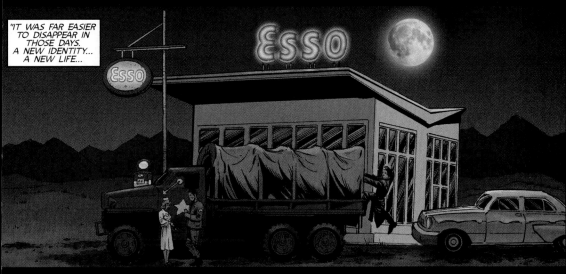

"IT WAS FAR EASIER TO DISAPPEAR IN THOSE DAYS. A NEW IDENTITY... A NEW LIFE...

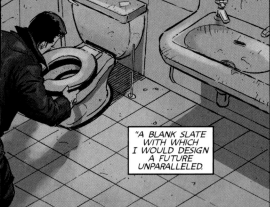

"A BLANK SLATE WITH WHICH I WOULD DESIGN A FUTURE UNPARALLELED.

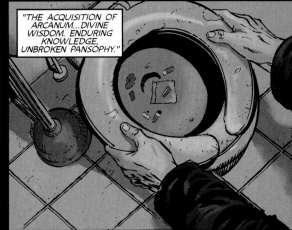

"THE ACQUISITION OF ARCANUM...DIVINE WISDOM. ENDURING KNOWLEDGE, UNBROKEN PANSOPHY."

CELESTIAL SUPREMACY.
I TRUST I'LL HAVE YOUR ANSWER BY TOMORROW?
YES, OF COURSE.
MR. THEAD?
MR. THEAD!
THANK YOU FOR COMING, MR. OSTMAN. I HAVE A GOOD FEELING ABOUT THIS. PLEASE...

OOOO... DON'T WE GOT HIM RIGHT WHERE WE WANT HIM, MR. THEAD? DIS HERE FURBALL ON THE **ROPES!**
WE KNOW WHAT DAT ANSWER GOING TO BE. YOU GONNA DO ALL MR. THEAD'S BIDDING NOW. THAT'S YOUR LOT NOW, SON!
MIND YOUR MANNERS NOW, MISS NESSIE. YOU CAN BE DEALT WITH RIGHT QUICK.
COME ON NOW. WE GOT PLACES TO BE. SAY, WHAT'S THAT OVER YON'? DON'T THAT LITTLE ONE LOOK FAMILIAR?

OH, WHAT A LOVELY TEA PARTY!
DADDY'S HOME!

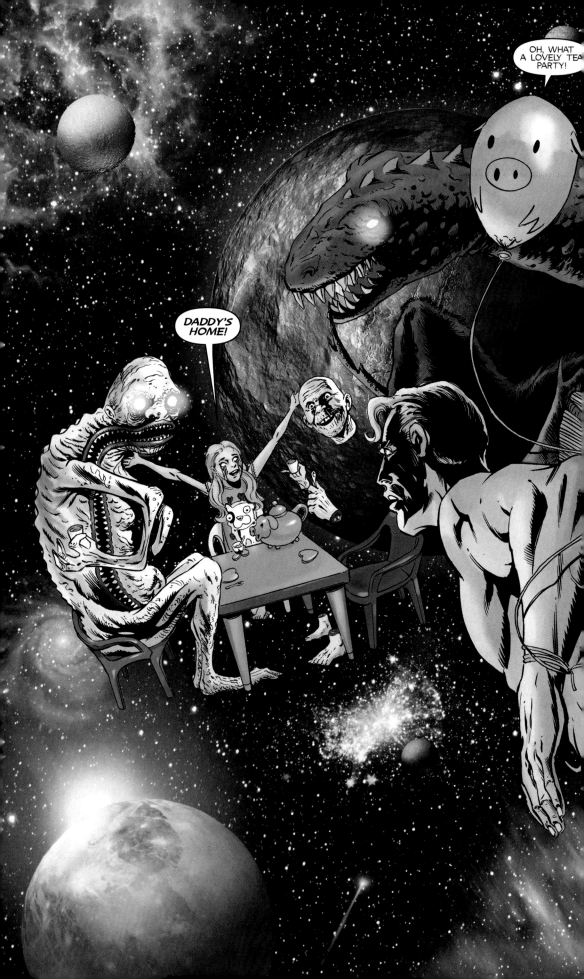

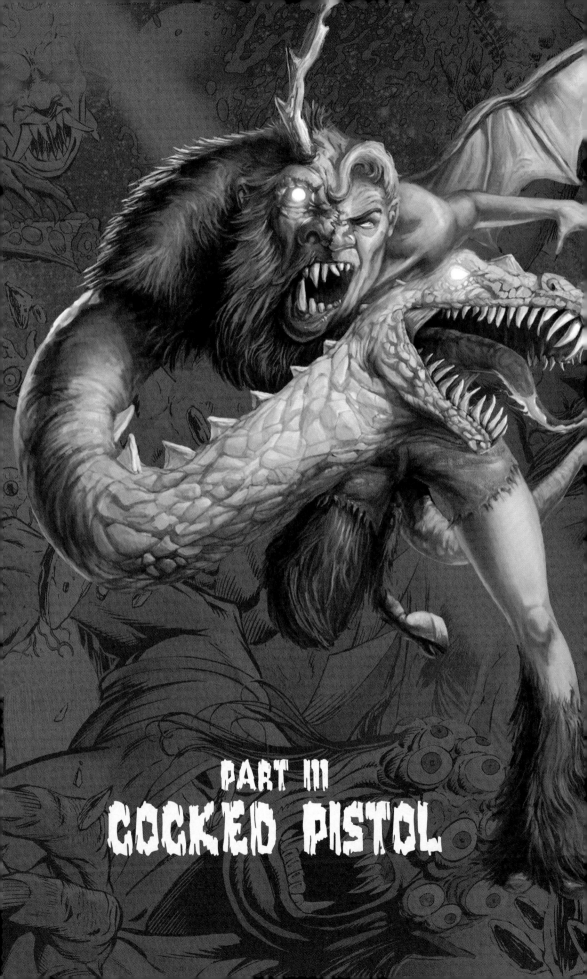

PART III
COCKED PISTOL

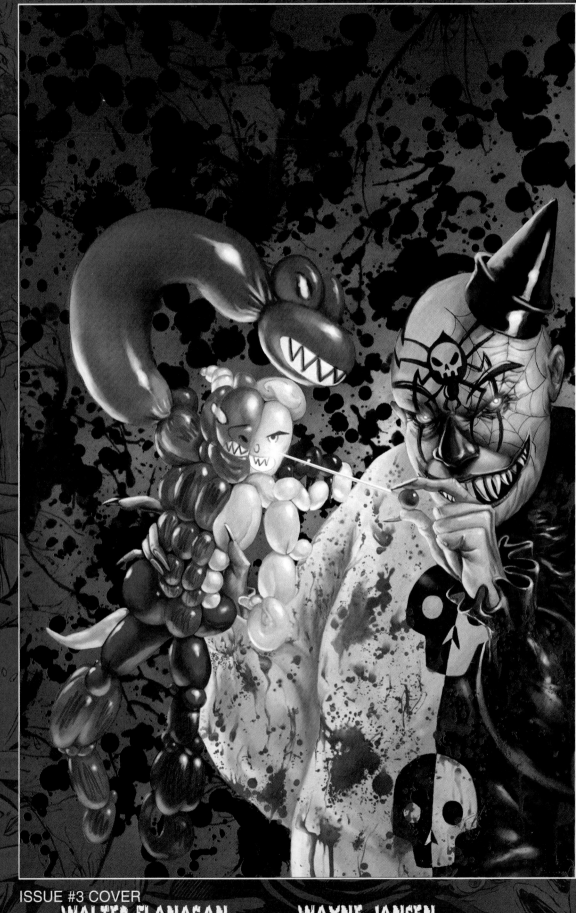

ISSUE #3 COVER
art by **WALTER FLANAGAN** colors by **WAYNE JANSEN**

CLOSER, CHILDREN. TAKE ME IN YOUR MOUTHS.
MAMA'S MILK'S GONNA SNUFF OUT THE FIRE THAT'S BEEN BURNING IN YOUR BELLIES.
LISTEN GOOD NOW, LI'L BABIES... WON'T BE LONG BEFORE TIME COMES FOR MAMA TO SHOW THE WORLD HER DREAMY TEETH AGAIN.
...WE ALL RECOLLECT WHAT HAPPENED LAST TIME. IN THAT PLACE WHERE THEM FOUR MET UP AFTER RUNNIN' ALL THAT WAY?
QUICK AS A BUNNY, UNBUTTONED ALL YOUR DADDY'S HARD WORK WITH ONE QUICK SHOT.
WASN'T HE CROSS? STOMPIN' ABOUT, SCARIN' THEM NICE FOLKS DOWN BELOW JUST ABOUT HALF TO DEATH.
SSSSSSS...
OH, THE RACKET HE MADE...

"I DIDN'T SEE MUCH OF THEAD AFTER OUR FIRST MEETING. ONCE, WHEN HE INTRODUCED ME TO MY ASSISTANT, GALE. NICE ENOUGH GUY. THE SECOND, AND LAST, WHEN HE EXPLAINED 'NIGHT SURF.'
"LAUGHABLE IN THEORY, PREPOSTEROUS IN EXECUTION. ONLY THE HEART OF A FOOL COULD BE STILLED IN FAITH.
"NIGHT SURF WOULD SEE A TEAM OF THEAD'S MAKING CAPTURE THE WORLD'S MOST ELUSIVE CRYPTIDS. MY LAB WAS CREATED FOR THE EXTRACTION OF--FOR LACK OF A BETTER WORD--THEIR SOULS.
"I WANTED MORE THAN ANYTHING TO PROVE THEAD'S THEORY THAT THE CRYPTIDS WERE PORTALS, BUT THE MORE DEEPLY I EXAMINED HIS WRITINGS...
"CASTLES IN THE AIR.
"BUT LIKE THE LADY ONCE SAID, THE THING WITH FEATHERS PERCHES IN THE SOUL.
"AS LONG AS SAMMI WANDERED THE HOLLOWS OF MY SPIRIT SINGING HER WORDLESS TUNE... I WOULD WAIT... AND I WOULD HOPE.
WE... WE DID IT! I CAN'T BELIEVE IT! IT'S...
"TIME PASSED. OUTSIDE THE WALLS, LEAVES TURNED AND FELL.
"THE SNOWS CAME...THEN THE MELT. LIFE PRESSED THROUGH, GREEN AND AMBITIOUS AND VIRGIN.
"ON A DAY NO DIFFERENT THAN THE HUNDREDS WHICH CAME BEFORE IT...
"WE SEPARATED THE BEAST FROM THE BEING."

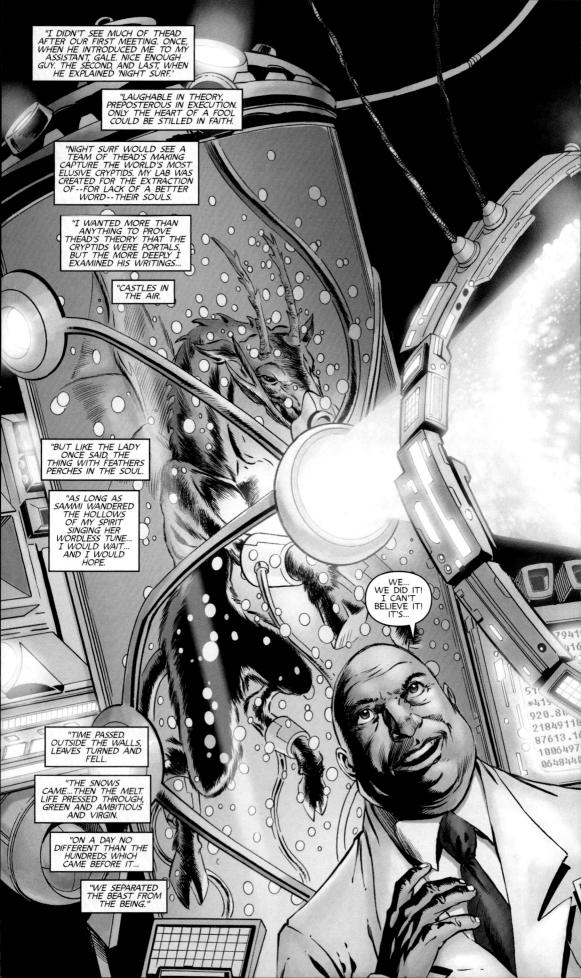

...EXQUISITE.

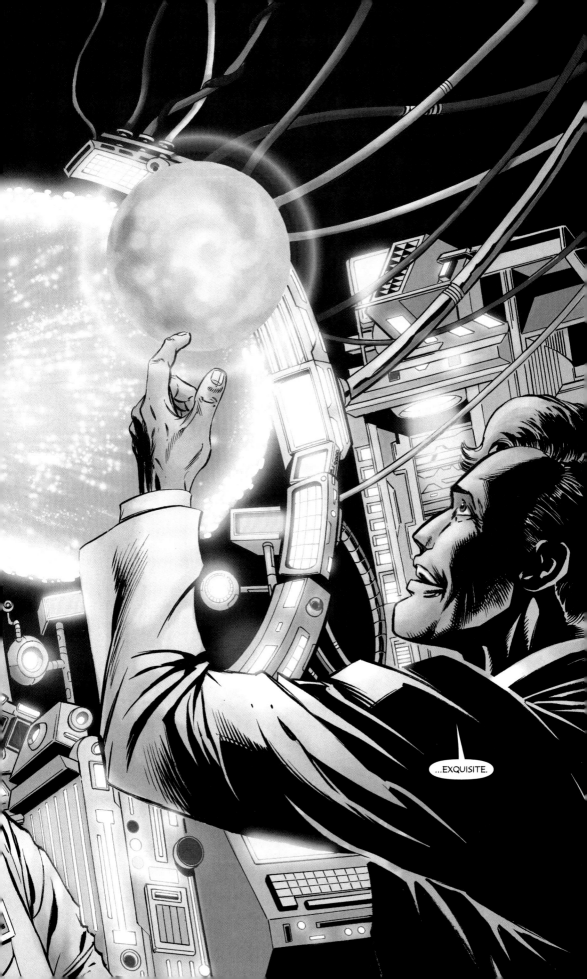

"IF THE CRYPTIDS WERE PATHWAYS TO DIFFERENT DIMENSIONS, COULDN'T THEY BE A GUIDE TO ANOTHER TIME?
WHERE DOES IT LEAD?
I DON'T KNOW YET.
"IF THAT TIME COULD BE ALTERED, REWRITTEN...
IT'S SO BRIGHT. LIKE...
DR. OSTMAN! GET DOWN!
"I'D SEEN THIS THING BEFORE.
"...IN A PLACE WHERE NO MATTER HOW BRIGHTLY THE SUN SHINES, THE SKY IS CHOKED AND DEAD.
WHA... WHAT IS THAT?!
"A SHAPELESS NIGHTMARE. THE PAIN OF THAT DAY IN THE WOODS ETCHED DEEP AND UNBROKEN.
I AM THE ONE WHO CARRIES THE MARK.
"IT WAS A THING THAT WORE A THOUSAND MASKS.
"EACH ONE UNSPEAKABLY HORRIFIC. EACH ONE AN INDICTMENT."
I AM...
...YOUR RUIN.

I AM LORD OVER THE INNOCENTS. RAPIST OF WITHERED SOULS THAT SUFFER COUNTLESS ETERNITIES IN ABJECT DESPAIR.
JOIN THEM!
AGGGHHHH!

MY GOD... GALE!
WHAT... DO YOU WANT?
YOU'VE ALREADY GIVEN US WHAT WE WANT, ALAN OSTMAN.
A WAY IN.

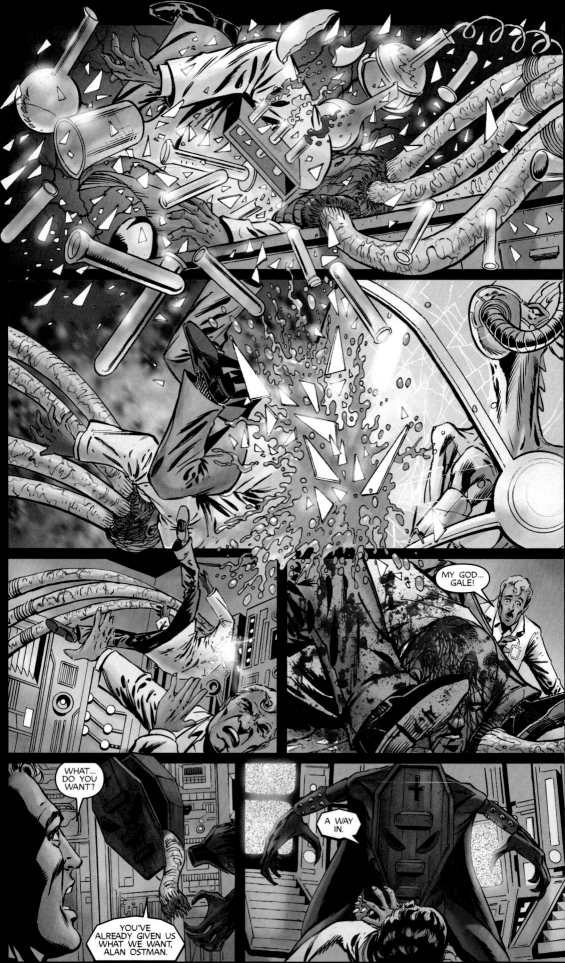

MINDLESS BEAST!
WHAT HAVE I DONE!?
DANGER DANGER DANGER
DANGER
WHAT THE HELL HAVE I DONE!?
"I STILL DON'T KNOW FOR WHOSE BENEFIT I SAID THOSE WORDS OUT LOUD. I KNEW EXACTLY WHAT I'D DONE.
"...AND WHY."

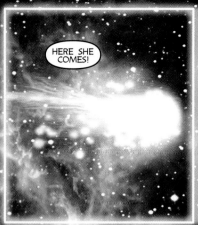

HERE SHE COMES!

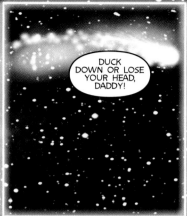

DUCK DOWN OR LOSE YOUR HEAD, DADDY!

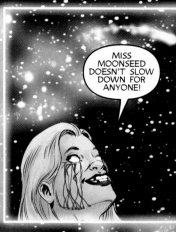

MISS MOONSEED DOESN'T SLOW DOWN FOR ANYONE!

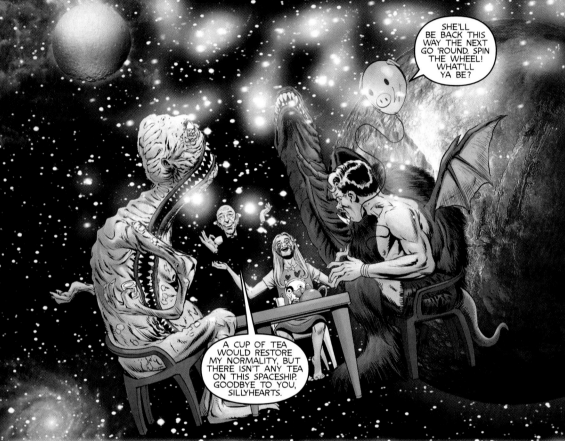

SHE'LL BE BACK THIS WAY THE NEXT GO 'ROUND. SPIN THE WHEEL! WHAT'LL YA BE?

A CUP OF TEA WOULD RESTORE MY NORMALITY, BUT THERE ISN'T ANY TEA ON THIS *SPACESHIP.* GOODBYE TO YOU, SILLYHEARTS.

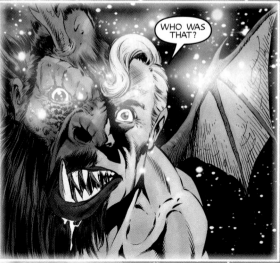

WHO WAS THAT?

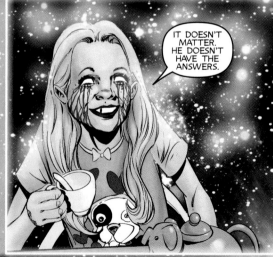

IT DOESN'T MATTER. HE DOESN'T HAVE THE ANSWERS.

WHY DON'T YOU TELL US WHO WE SHOULD BE ASKIN', LITTLE ONE?
DO YOU WANT TO KNOW SOMETHING ABOUT MY DADDY? SOMETHING SUPER SECRET?
HOW I LOVE THE CONSPIRATORIAL. DO TELL.
A LONG TIME AGO, BEFORE MY MOMMY KILLED HERSELF...
STAY AWAY FROM HER!
DADDY! NO! BE NICE!
I WAS GOING TO TELL HIM THAT SOMETIMES YOU WOULD TRY TO MAKE MOMMY CRY ON PURPOSE, BECAUSE YOU ALWAYS THOUGHT HER EYES LOOKED PRETTIEST WHEN SHE CRIED.
THAT WASN'T WHAT YOU WERE GOING TO SAY, WAS IT?

MOSTLY EVERYONE CALLS THEM "THE HOSTILES." IT'S THEIR REAL NAME. I CALL THEM THE MONSTER PEOPLE, AND THEY'RE ANGRY, DADDY. THEY'VE ALWAYS BEEN SO ANGRY.
"THEY COME FROM A PLACE WHERE EVERYTHING IS DARK EXCEPT FOR THE FIRE IN THE SKY.
"THE MONSTER PEOPLE WERE MADE...DIFFERENT. NOT ON PURPOSE, BUT LIKE WHEN A SCULPTOR PRACTICES AND HIS STATUE ISN'T...RIGHT.
"DO YOU REMEMBER MOMMY'S LITTLE NESTING DOLLS? THE ONES HER GRANDPA BOUGHT SO SHE WOULDN'T TELL ABOUT THE TIMES HE TOOK HER TO THE PARKING LOT BEHIND THE OLD PAINT FACTORY?
"SOMETIMES ONE OF THEM IS IN THE RIGHT PLACE AT THE RIGHT TIME.
"THEY GET TO LEAVE THE PLACE THEY HATE SO MUCH JUST FOR A LITTLE WHILE.

"WHAT THEY HATE, WHAT THEY REALLY HATE, IS THAT THEY'RE SO CLOSE TO GETTING OUT.
"THEIR GRANDPAS BUILT A TRIANGLE A LONG, LONG TIME AGO, BUT THEY ONLY KNOW HOW TO PULL PEOPLE IN.
"THE MONSTER PEOPLE NEED BADNESS TO HAPPEN. LIKE WHEN A LOT OF SOULS GO MISSING ALL AT THE SAME TIME.
"THEY LIKE TO KILL EVEN THE GENTLEST CREATURES. IT MAKES THE BLACKEST PARTS OF THEIR INSIDES DANCE.
"THEY ALWAYS TRY TO BRING PEOPLE BACK WITH THEM SO THEY CAN TURN THEM INTO MONSTER PEOPLE JUST LIKE THEM.
YOU'RE MY...YOU'RE MY LITTLE GIRL. WHY DO YOU KNOW THIS? WHY ARE YOU TELLING ME?

"BECAUSE THE NEXT TIME YOU DREAM, IT MIGHT NOT BE OF ME.
"DO WE ALL LIVE IN THE DREAM, DADDY?"
"SOME OF US DIE IN IT."
"I THINK SOME PEOPLE HIDE SO DEEP EVEN THEIR SHADOW GETS LOST.
"THERE'S A MAN WHO SNEAKS INTO A PERSON'S BODY AND TAKES IT."
"TAKES WHAT?"
"HE USES THE SHADOW TO HELP THE MONSTER PEOPLE. HE CAN OPEN DOORWAYS AND MAKE THEM STAY OPEN.
"BUT BEFORE HE CAN DO THAT, HE NEEDS TO KILL ALL THE ANGEL BABIES.
"I'M SORRY, MISS NESSIE. I DIDN'T MEAN TO SCARE YOU.
CHILD, PAY NO HEED TO THE YOWLING OF THAT CREATURE.
"IT'S WHY THE ANGELS NEED YOU...

"...THE ALIENS WHO MADE YOU."
"WHAT DO YOU MEAN?"
"THEIR BABIES ARE HOW THE ANGELS GET PLACES. THEY'RE SHORTCUTS TO ANYWHERE THE ANGELS WANT TO GO.
"THE SHADOW MAN WANTS TO TAKE THE SHORTCUTS FOR HIMSELF."
"THAT'S ALL?"
"NO.

"EVERY TIME HE KILLS A BABY HE...EATS A PIECE OF THEM."
"WHAT?!"
"HE EATS PART OF THE BABY."
"WHA...WHY?"
"HE SAYS TO CONSECRATE AND CONSUME THE FLESH OF A BABY IS TO COME CLOSER TO BECOMING GOD."
"THIS SHADOW MAN, HE'S INSANE."

"HE IS, BUT HE'S ALSO RIGHT.
"HE'S GOING TO COMPLETE THE CIRCLE OF THE SIX. ALL HE NEEDS ARE SIX BABIES TO..."
"DESTROY THE WORLD?"
"NOT JUST THE WORLD, DADDY. EVERYTHING.

"HE WANTS THERE TO BE...NOTHING."

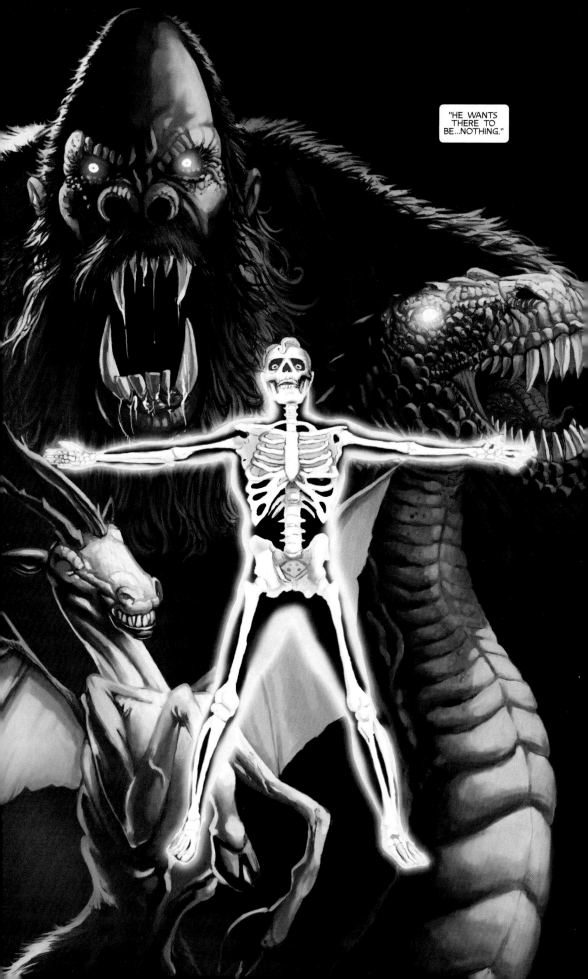

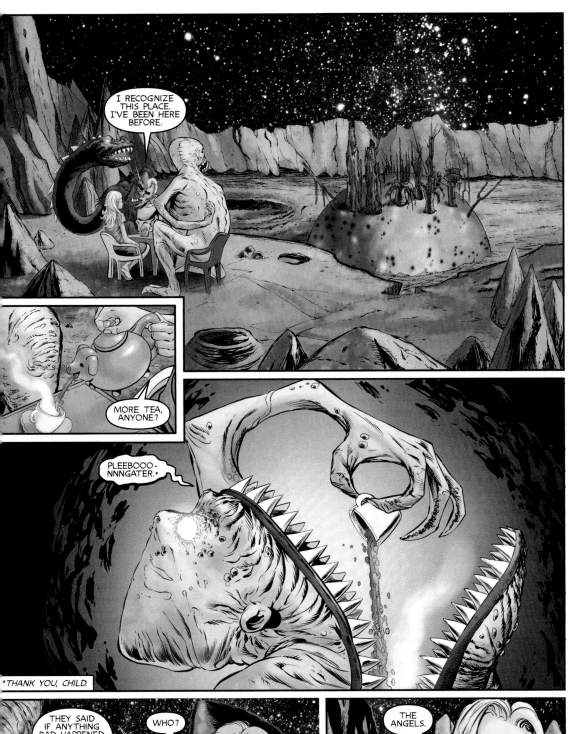

I RECOGNIZE THIS PLACE. I'VE BEEN HERE BEFORE.

MORE TEA, ANYONE?

PLEEBOOO - NNNGATER.*

*THANK YOU, CHILD.

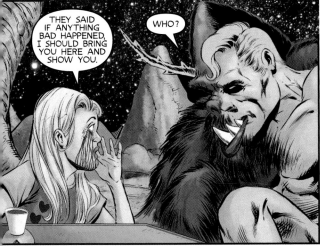

THEY SAID IF ANYTHING BAD HAPPENED, I SHOULD BRING YOU HERE AND SHOW YOU.

WHO?

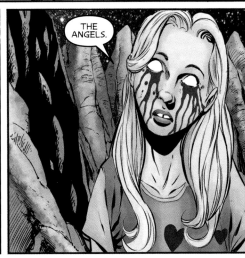

THE ANGELS.

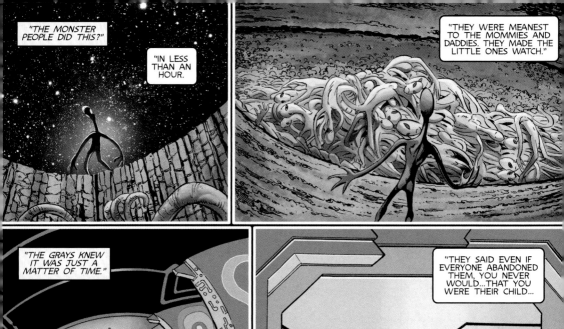

"THE MONSTER PEOPLE DID THIS?"

"IN LESS THAN AN HOUR."

"THEY WERE MEANEST TO THE MOMMIES AND DADDIES. THEY MADE THE LITTLE ONES WATCH."

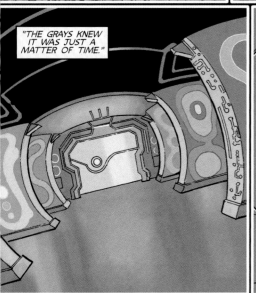

"THE GRAYS KNEW IT WAS JUST A MATTER OF TIME."

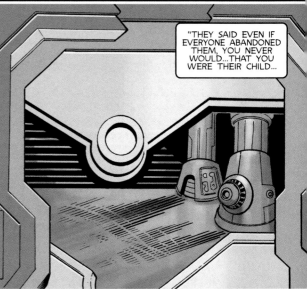

"THEY SAID EVEN IF EVERYONE ABANDONED THEM, YOU NEVER WOULD...THAT YOU WERE THEIR CHILD..."

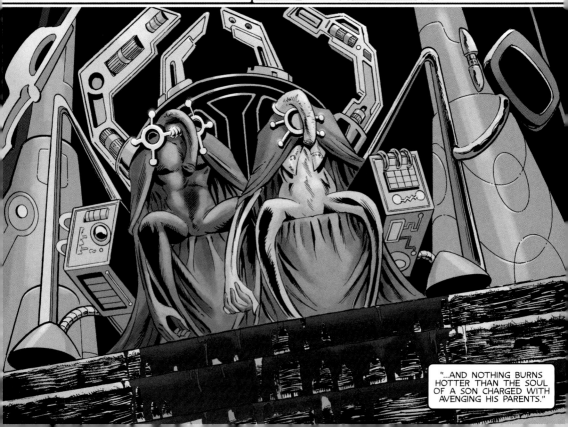

"...AND NOTHING BURNS HOTTER THAN THE SOUL OF A SON CHARGED WITH AVENGING HIS PARENTS."

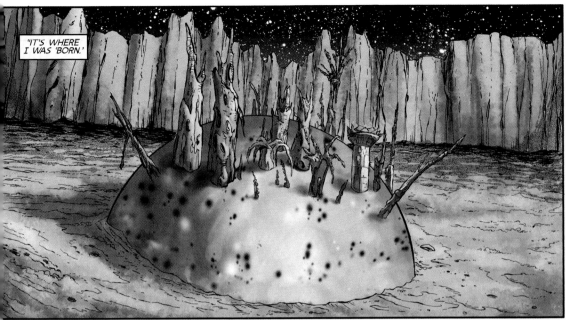

"IT'S WHERE I WAS 'BORN.'"

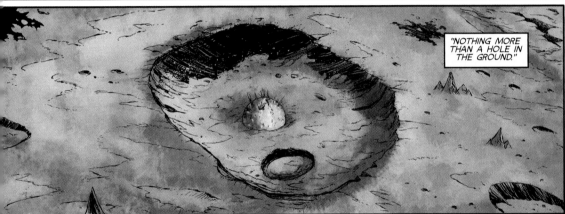

"NOTHING MORE THAN A HOLE IN THE GROUND."

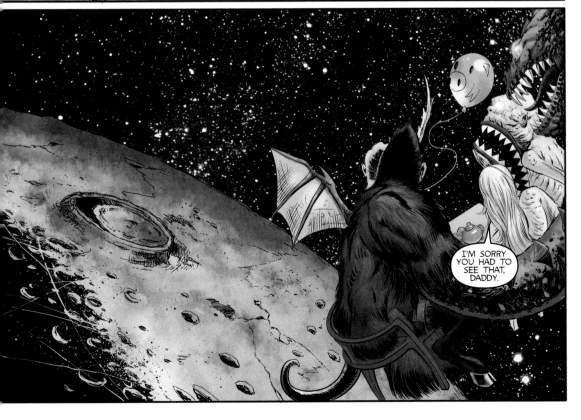

I'M SORRY YOU HAD TO SEE THAT, DADDY.

WELL DON'T WE HAVE OUR WORK CUT OUT FOR US?
I'LL HELP YOU FIGHT THE MONSTER PEOPLE, DADDY.
PLEE-TOOK ARIANA.*
*HOW SWEET.
TACKAFO-SWEEDIDDLE.*
*IN ANOTHER LIFE THAT SENTIMENT MAY WELL HAVE SEEN PRINT ON THE FRONT OF A GREETING CARD.
SAMMI, BACK AWAY FROM IT!

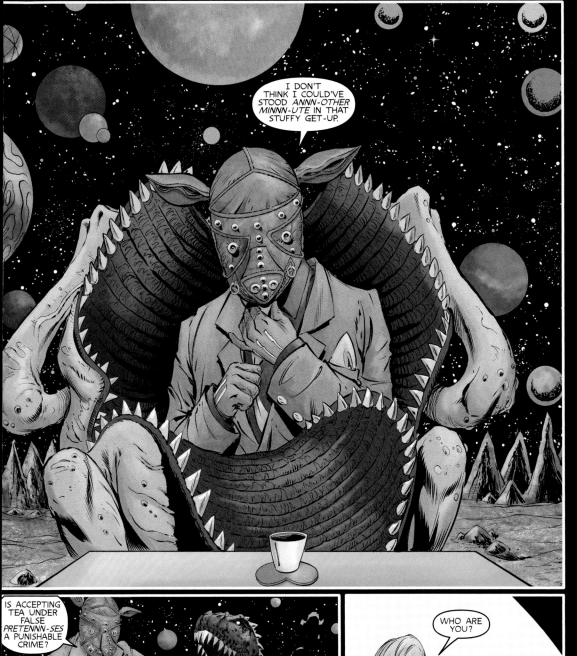

I DON'T THINK I COULD'VE STOOD *ANN-OTHER MINNN-UTE* IN THAT STUFFY GET-UP.

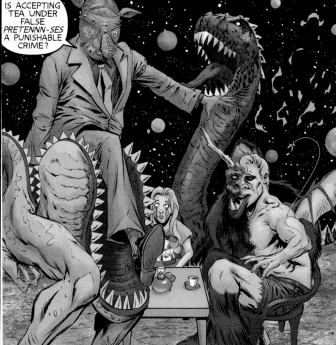

IS ACCEPTING TEA UNDER FALSE *PRETENNN-SES* A PUNISHABLE CRIME?

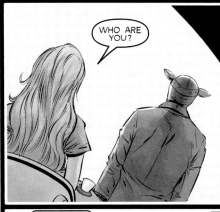

WHO ARE YOU?

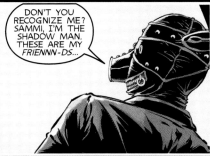

DON'T YOU RECOGNIZE ME? SAMMI, I'M THE SHADOW MAN. THESE ARE MY *FRIENNN-DS...*

...AND THEY ARE THE BEGINNING OF THE *ENNN-D*.

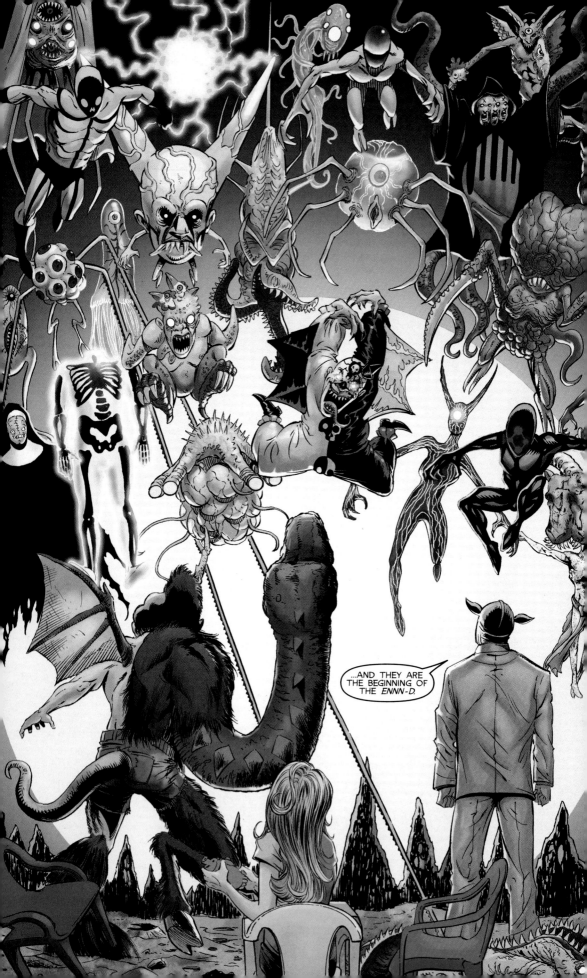

PART IV
FAIL DEADLY

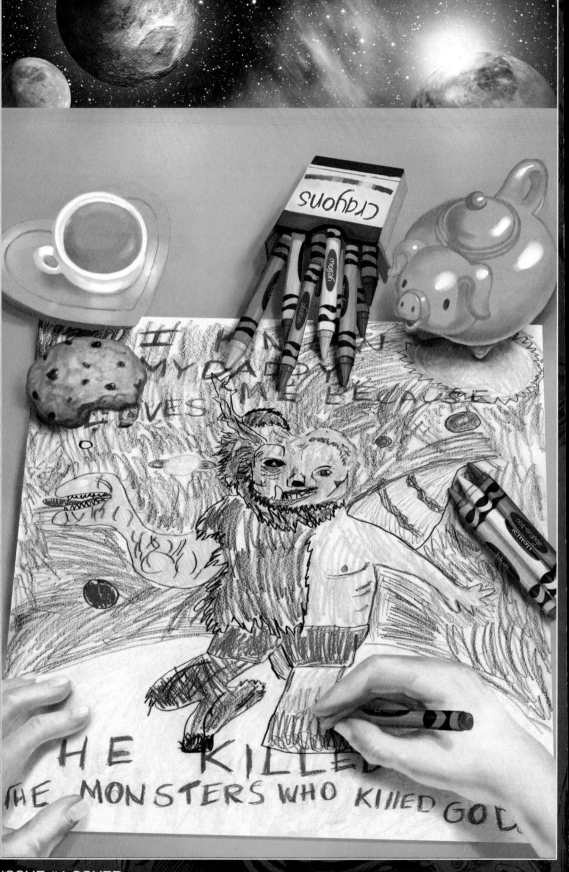

ISSUE #4 COVER
art by WALTER FLANAGAN and ALICIA FLANAGAN

"DID MY LITTLE GIRL DREAM OF HOT SUPPER?
"LISTEN FOR THE CHIME OF THE THIRTEENTH?
"DID SHE CRY POOLS OF TEARS?
"BLUE FIRES BLAZING IN HER EYES.
"A LIFE TO COME, UNVEILED.
"A THOUSAND YEARS UPON US.

"AND WITH IT, FINAL JUDGEMENT."
PUPPY WUV

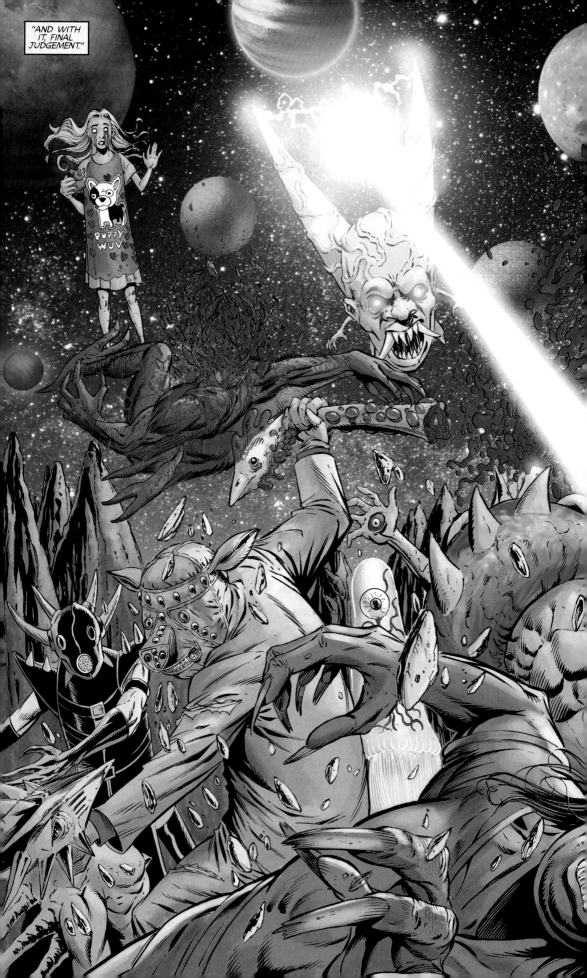

"DO YOU KNOW THAT I NEVER STOPPED LOOKING..."
DADDY! LOOK OUT BEHIND YOU!
AGGGHHHH!
"NEVER STOPPED WONDERING..."
THERE ARE...TOO MANY!
I'LL GET HIM.
LEAVE MY DADDY...
"...OR MISSING YOU."
...ALONE!
"COULD YOU KNOW THAT WHEN YOUR MOTHER TOOK HER OWN LIFE..."
WE CAN'T WIN, DADDY.
"HOW DESPERATELY I WANTED TO FOLLOW? IN THE END, IT WAS THE TERROR THAT STAYED ME.
"THE PROFOUND DREAD OF YOUR RETURN..."
NOT LIKE THIS.

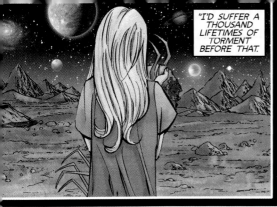

"I'D SUFFER A THOUSAND LIFETIMES OF TORMENT BEFORE THAT.

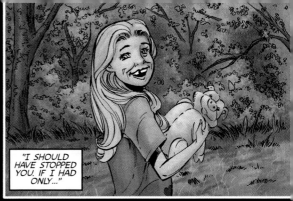

"I SHOULD HAVE STOPPED YOU. IF I HAD ONLY..."

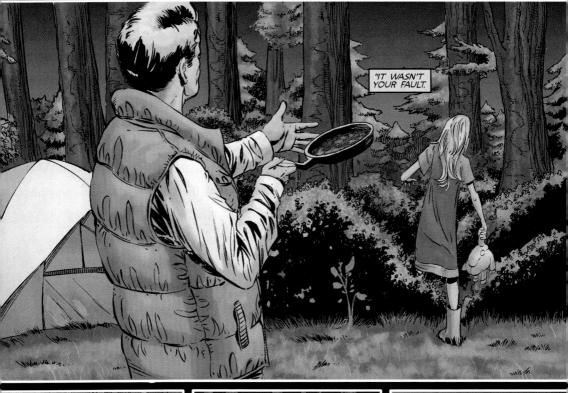

"IT WASN'T YOUR FAULT.

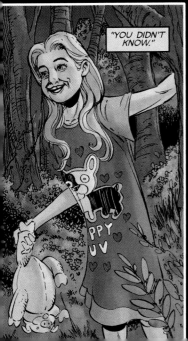

"YOU DIDN'T KNOW."

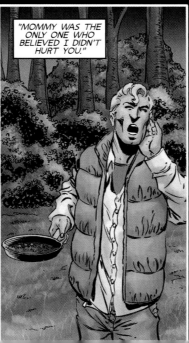

"MOMMY WAS THE ONLY ONE WHO BELIEVED I DIDN'T HURT YOU."

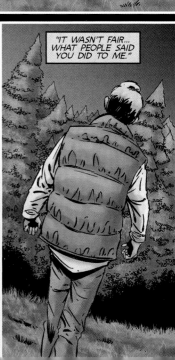

"IT WASN'T FAIR... WHAT PEOPLE SAID YOU DID TO ME."

"I DON'T KNOW HOW, BUT WHEN I SAW FERN ON THE GROUND I KNEW..."
"I WAS GONE?"
"YES.
"ALL I REMEMBER WAS..."
"THE LIGHT."
"IT WAS SO BRIGHT, BUT...COLD."

DADDY...
I...
CAN'T...
...SEE YOU!

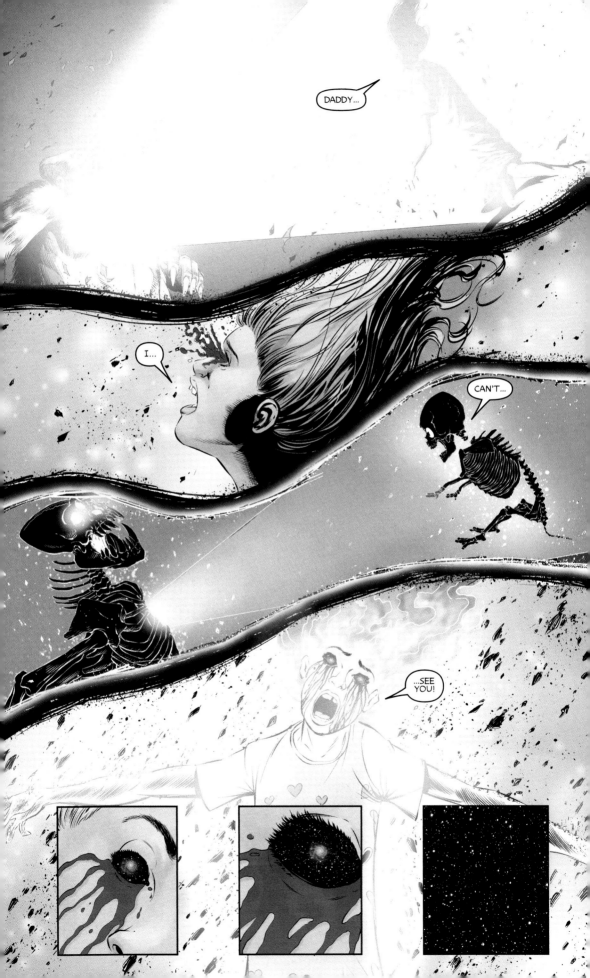

"WE WEREN'T SUPPOSED TO BE THERE THAT DAY.
OPIE'S
B-B-Q
"IT'S WHY THE ANGELS CHOSE YOU."
"BECAUSE I HAD NOTHING? I **WAS** NOTHING?"
"THEY KNEW WHAT YOU HAD LOST...
OPIE'S
B-B-Q
"...AND WHAT YOU WOULD DO TO GET ME BACK."

THE LIGHT IS...THE LIGHT IS TOO LOUD. IT...
IT... WHAT THE %#$^?!
WHAT ARE YOU?!

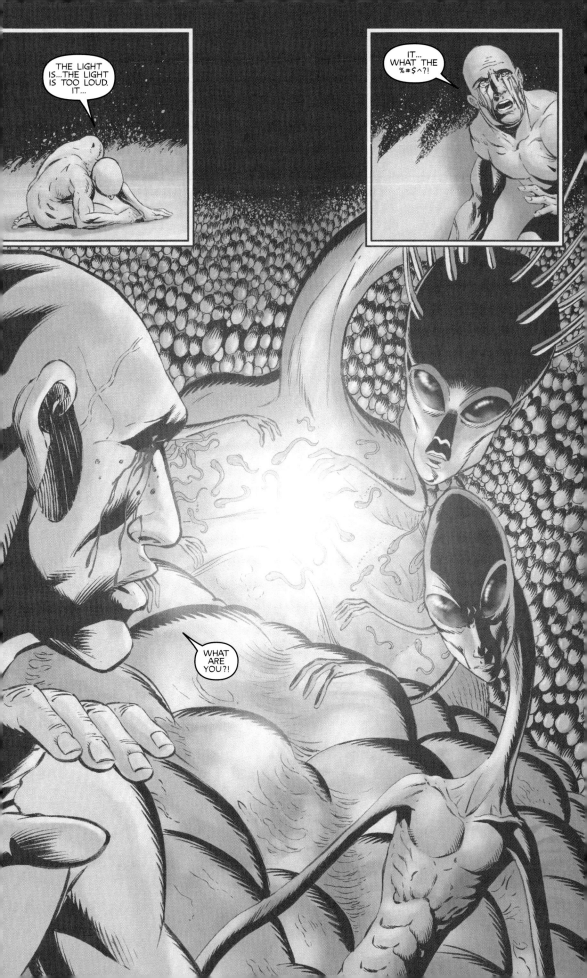

WHAT DO YOU WANT!?
DO YOU WANT HER BACK, OSTMAN?
WHA...
DO YOU WANT YOUR LITTLE ONE? YOUR SAMMI?
SAMMI
SAMMI
SAMMI
SAMMI
EEEYYYAH!
SAMMI
ARE YOU PREPARED TO GIVE OF YOURSELF, OSTMAN, FOR HER? TO SACRIFICE WHAT YOU CAN NEVER RECLAIM?
YES... ANYTHING.

ANYTHING.
"THEN OPEN YOURSELF TO WHAT NEEDS TO HAPPEN. TO FIGHT IS TO BETRAY HER. THERE'S ONLY ONE WAY.
"LET THEM DO THEIR WORK, OSTMAN. LET THEM INSIDE YOU... UNTIL YOUR SOUL IS PIERCED AND YOUR HUMANITY EXPELLED."
IT'LL BE OVER SOON, DADDY.
PUPPY WUV
SAMMI?
PUPPY WUV

WHAT HAVE THEY DONE TO YOU?
THEY SHOWED ME...LIKE THEY'RE GOING TO SHOW YOU.
SHOW ME WHAT?
A WAY OUT.
NO, SAMMI! THEY LIED TO YOU!
THAT IS NOT THE LIE, DADDY!
THIS...
THIS IS THE LIE!

AND *HE* IS THE LIAR!
UPPY WUV
LOOK AT WHAT THEY'VE *DONNN-E* TO YOUR BELOVED!

NO!
FIRST YOU WILL ANSWER FOR YOUR SINS, PIGMAN.
PUPPY WUV

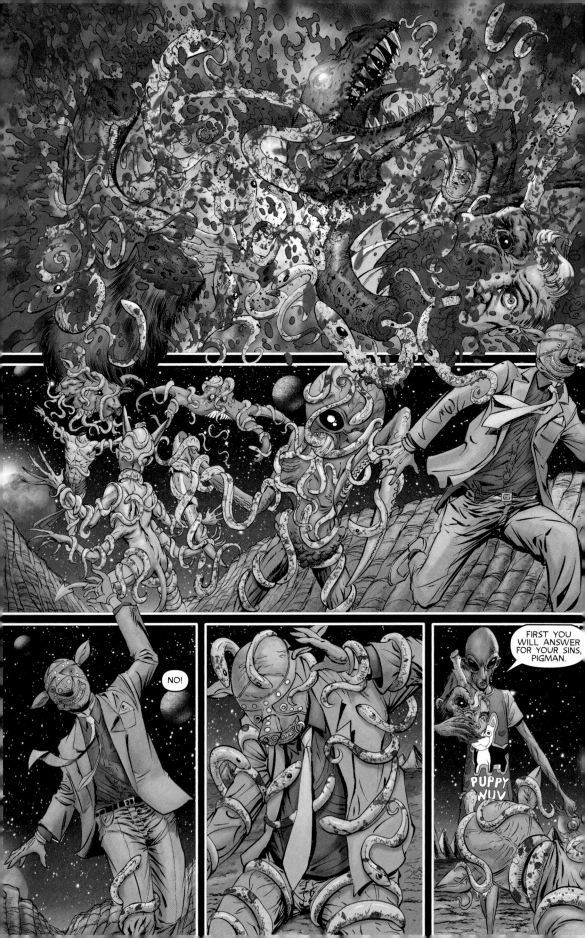

TELL MY DADDY WHY THE ANGELS WANT HIM TO KILL YOU.
TELL HIM!
"SOME MEN ARE ARTISTS.
"OTHERS, THE CANNN-VAS.
"WITH YOUR HELP, I PAINNN-TED THE WORLD'S FUTURE IN THE BLOOD OF INNN-OCENTS."

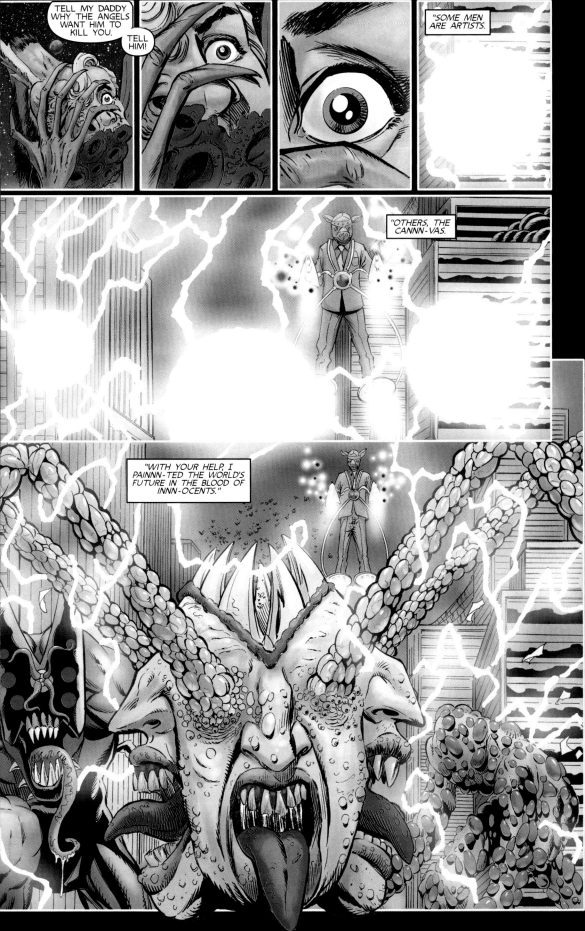

"DO YOU KNOW HOW LONG YOU WAGED THE UNWINN-NABLE BATTLE, MONNN-STER?"
WHAT DO YOU MEAN?
THE DAY WILL COME WHEN I PLUCK YOU FROM THE DEPTHS AND YOU WILL LEARN THE MEANING OF AGONY.
LOOK AROUND, YOU MONSTER! DO YOU SEE THE DEATH? THE DEVASTATION? WHAT IS IT IF NOT THE SACRIFICE OF THOUSANDS TO SATE THE SINGLEMINDED OBSESSION OF RECLAIMING YOUR BLOOD?
ONCE THE CODE WAS DECIPHERED, IT WAS *YOU* WHO OPENED THE PORTALS AND GAVE ENTRY TO THESE CREATURES.
THE MONSTER PEOPLE, I BELIEVE YOUR LITTLE ONE CALLS THEM.
YOU ARE THE LAST *MONNN-STER*. YOUR CRYPTID BRETHRENNN WHO LIVED FOR THOUSANNN-DS OF YEARS AS LEGEND...ARE DEAD BY THE HAND OF YOUR HUMAN FORM.
NO! I DIDN'T KILL THEM! I...
LEFT THE DOORWAYS *UNNN*-GUARDED...FOR *ETERNNN-ITY*. THOSE WHO WOULD RAVAGE *EVERYTHINNN-G*, NOW HOLD FREE *REIG-NNN*.

NO... I DIDN'T.
"THE ORBS ARE INFINITE, MONN-STER. THE PORTALS, A TEAR BETWEEN OURS AND THE NIGHTMARE DIMENSION!
"BECAUSE OF YOU, GOOD AND EVIL HAVE BECOME ONE."
DON'T LISTEN TO HIM, DADDY!
DON'T LISTEN! IT'S NOT TRUE! THERE'S A WAY WE CAN CHANGE...
PUPP
WUV
STAY AWAY!
NO!
GWORK!
DADDY!

GIVE...HIM... BACK!!
ARE YOU OKAY, DADDY?
WHAT'S HAPPENING?
WHY AM I STILL ALIVE? HOW...
SHHH... IT'S OKAY.

IF YOU WANT, YOU CAN COME WITH ME.
WHERE?
HOME.
HOME?
IT'S IN HERE. RIGHT INSIDE THE TEAPOT THE ANGELS GAVE TO ME. THEY SAID IT'S THE LAST WORLD. EVERYBODY'S LAST CHANCE.
WE CAN GO RIGHT NOW AND EVERYTHING WOULD BE JUST LIKE IT USED TO BE...BEFORE ALL THE BAD THINGS STARTED HAPPENING.
WE COULD GO CAMPING IN OUR FAVORITE SPOT IN HARTSHORNE WOODS.
...AND FEED THAT FUNNY LOOKING GOOSE WHO ALWAYS BULLIES THE POOR DUCKS DOWN AT MONTGOMERY POND.
...AND WE'D SEE MOMMY AGAIN.
HOW?

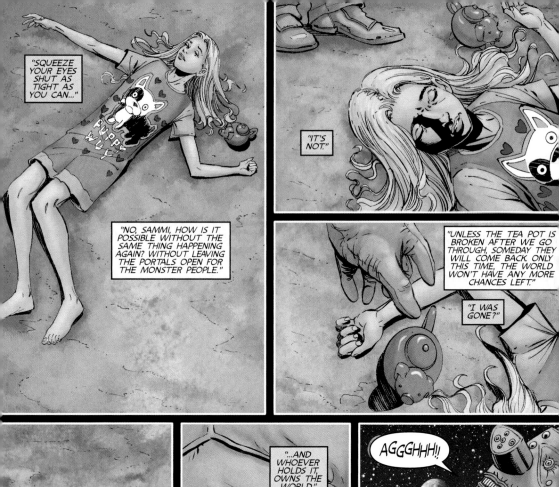

"SQUEEZE YOUR EYES SHUT AS TIGHT AS YOU CAN..."

"IT'S NOT."

"NO, SAMMI, HOW IS IT POSSIBLE WITHOUT THE SAME THING HAPPENING AGAIN? WITHOUT LEAVING THE PORTALS OPEN FOR THE MONSTER PEOPLE."

"UNLESS THE TEA POT IS BROKEN AFTER WE GO THROUGH, SOMEDAY THEY WILL COME BACK. ONLY THIS TIME, THE WORLD WON'T HAVE ANY MORE CHANCES LEFT."

"I WAS GONE?"

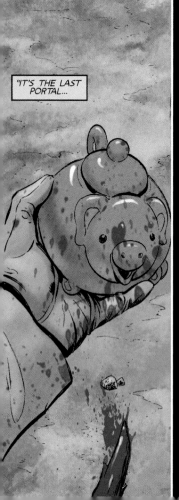

"IT'S THE LAST PORTAL...

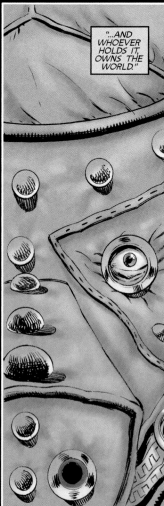

"...AND WHOEVER HOLDS IT, OWNS THE WORLD."

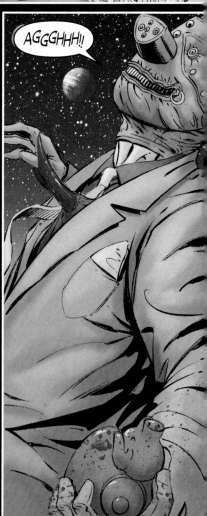

AGGGHHH!!

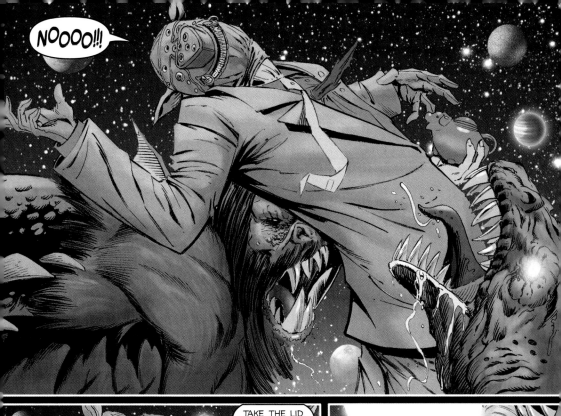

NOOOO!!!

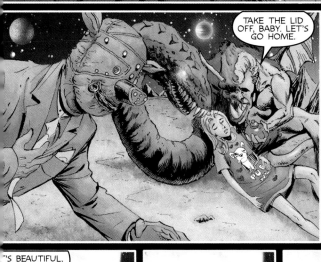

TAKE THE LID OFF, BABY. LET'S GO HOME.

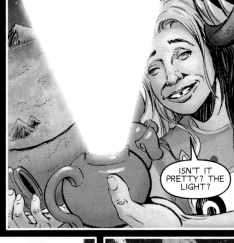

ISN'T IT PRETTY? THE LIGHT?

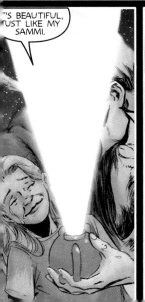

'S BEAUTIFUL, 'UST LIKE MY SAMMI.

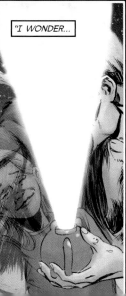

"I WONDER...

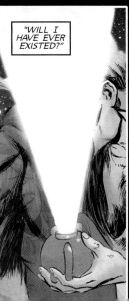

"WILL I HAVE EVER EXISTED?"

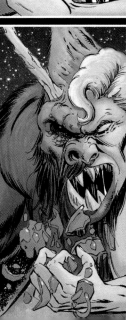

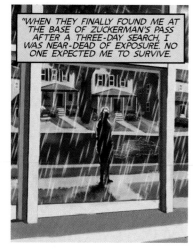

"WHEN THEY FINALLY FOUND ME AT THE BASE OF ZUCKERMAN'S PASS AFTER A THREE-DAY SEARCH, I WAS NEAR-DEAD OF EXPOSURE. NO ONE EXPECTED ME TO SURVIVE.

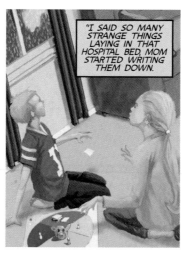

"I SAID SO MANY STRANGE THINGS LAYING IN THAT HOSPITAL BED. MOM STARTED WRITING THEM DOWN.

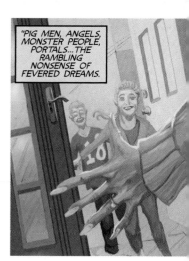

"PIG MEN, ANGELS, MONSTER PEOPLE, PORTALS...THE RAMBLING NONSENSE OF FEVERED DREAMS.

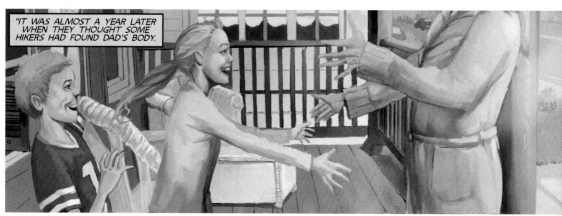

"IT WAS ALMOST A YEAR LATER WHEN THEY THOUGHT SOME HIKERS HAD FOUND DAD'S BODY.

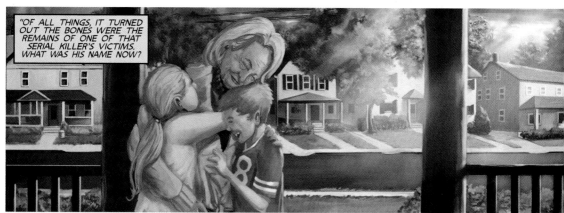

"OF ALL THINGS, IT TURNED OUT THE BONES WERE THE REMAINS OF ONE OF THAT SERIAL KILLER'S VICTIMS. WHAT WAS HIS NAME NOW?

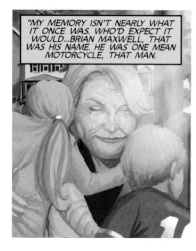

"MY MEMORY ISN'T NEARLY WHAT IT ONCE WAS. WHO'D EXPECT IT WOULD...BRIAN MAXWELL, THAT WAS HIS NAME. HE WAS ONE MEAN MOTORCYCLE, THAT MAN.

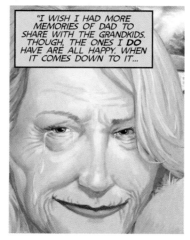

"I WISH I HAD MORE MEMORIES OF DAD TO SHARE WITH THE GRANDKIDS. THOUGH, THE ONES I DO HAVE ARE ALL HAPPY. WHEN IT COMES DOWN TO IT...

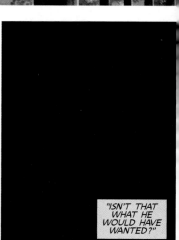

"ISN'T THAT WHAT HE WOULD HAVE WANTED?"

End...?

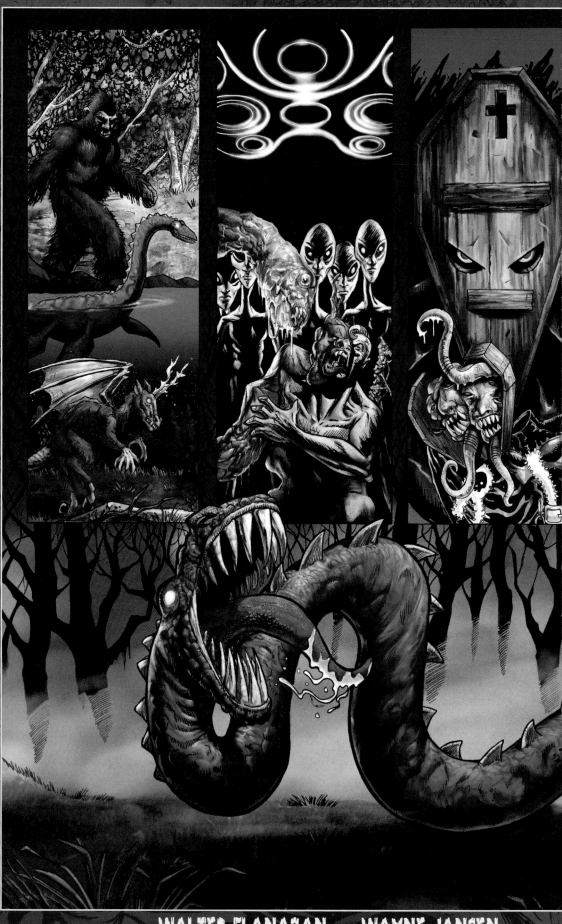

Original proposal art by **WALTER FLANAGAN** and **WAYNE JANSEN**

PUPPY WUV
THE
CRYPTOZOIC
MAN

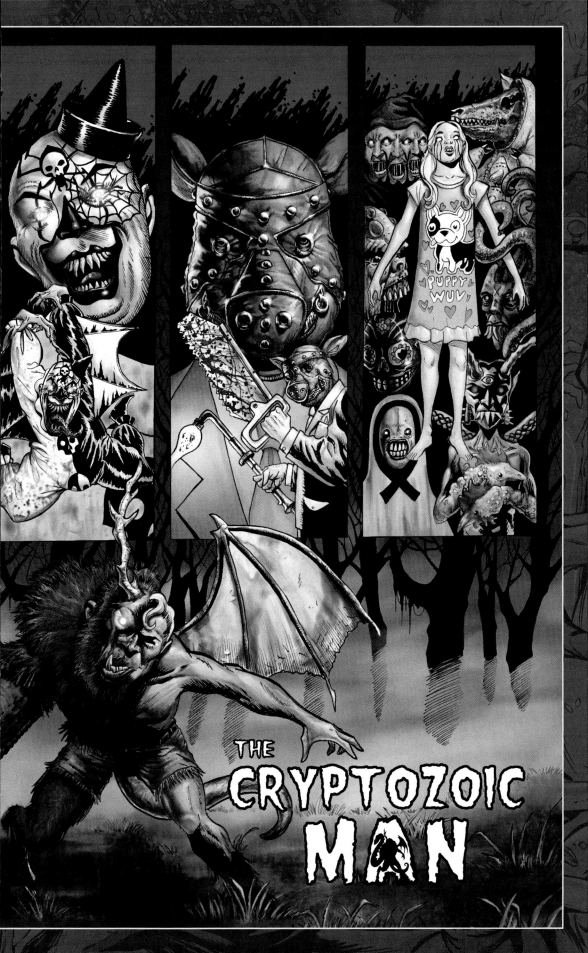

CRYPTOZOIC MAN ISSUE ONE

<u>PAGE ONE</u>

PANEL ONE

EXT. SUBURBAN NEIGHBORHOOD - PORCH - DAY

A WOMAN stands on the front porch of a house looking outwards to a suburban neighborhood.

> DIALOGUE BOX (upper left corner)
> These Hungry Ghosts who walk amongst us. Their waking lives long atrophied...their promise abandoned...

> DIALOGUE BOX (lower right corner)
> ...content to suffer fragmented truths until oblivion, and along with it, the dream's end.

PANEL TWO

EXT. SUBURBAN NEIGHBORHOOD - YARD - DAY

A DOG lies at the feet of an elderly WOMAN.

> DIALOGUE BOX (upper left corner)
> Mrs. Hammond was scolding Brantford for routing about in her tulip bed. Her eyes weren't what they once were...

DIALOGUE BOX (lower right corner)
> ...or she'd have noticed the sudden crimson rim of the horizon.

PANEL THREE

EXT. SUBURBAN NEIGHBORHOOD - SIDEWALK - DAY

Wider shot of a MAN riding an ADULT TRICYCLE with a folded up newspaper in his hand ready to toss. Panel includes Mrs. Schroeder IN BG.

> DIALOGUE BOX (upper left corner)
> Eddie 'Bug-Turd'. A newspaper 'boy' who had three drug induced strokes by the time he turned thirty-one was running behind on deliveries.

> DIALOGUE BOX (lower right corner)
> If anyone cared enough to ask him why, he'd have told them his mom 'messed with his sneakers'.

PANEL FOUR

EXT. SUBURBAN NEIGHBORHOOD - A WINDOW - DAY

A WOMAN draws a curtain across the window. A MAN stands behind her with his hands on her shoulders.

> DIALOGUE BOX (upper left corner)
> Thin veneer of pretense lends readily to delusion. ~~That~~ In the rippling currents of the rueful stream, regard exists...

> DIALOGUE BOX (lower right corner)
> ...that somehow, an adulteress would be favored above the flotsam of humanity.

PANEL FIVE/SIX/SEVEN

EXT. SUBURBAN NEIGHBORHOOD - DAY

Long panel broken (ragged edges) into three separate images of Mrs. Schroeder, Eddie 'bug-turd', and the adulteress.

> DIALOGUE BOX (Mrs. Hammond)
> Pride.

> DIALOGUE BOX (Eddie Jeffries)
> Gluttony.

> DIALOGUE BOX (Cheating Spouse)
> Lust.

PANEL EIGHT

Long Panel. Weird "Tales From the Darkside" vibe.

> DIALOGUE BOX (upper left corner)
> John of Patmos was right. The sun became black as sackcloth and the vials of ~~the~~ wrath were poured upon the earth.

> DIALOGUE BOX (lower right corner)
> ...but it had nothing to do with The Lord.

PAGES TWO/THREE - SPLASH PAGE

FOLLOWING TEXT ACROSS BOTH PAGES
PART I
DECAPITATION STRIKE

EXT. CITY BLOCK - DAY

Cars overturned and burning. Windows of nearby buildings are shattered. The sky is a gunmetal gray. Ash floats in the air and blankets the surface of anything flat. Post-apocalyptic, Road Warrior feel.

THE CRYPTOZOIC MAN (known as CMan from here on for sake of brevity) battles a CREATURE in the middle of the intersection. A second, bloody and dead CREATURE hangs from the mouth of THE LOCH NESS MONSTER (CMan's arm).

A third CREATURE emerges from a manhole cover.

PAGE FOUR

EXT. CITY BLOCK - DAY

PANEL ONE

Shoulders up on CMan roaring.

CMAN (dialogue box upper left corner)
In another life, I was Alan Ostman. I had a wife and a daughter,
and we lived in a postage-stamp of a town in Washington State.

CMAN (ldialogue box lower right corner)
Last Spring I thought I might even run for council...I never did get the
chance.

PANEL TWO

Closer on CMan's face.

CMAN (dialogue box upper left corner)
Has it been a week since I became *this*?A month? A year? Time passes
without notice.

CMAN (dialogue box lower right corner)
Near the end, when I was still Alan Ostman, I sometimes heard people
call it the after-times.

PANEL THREE

ECU on CMan's eye.

CMAN (dialogue box upper left corner)
What they meant was after The Hostiles murdered God, then burned
heaven and everything in it.

ALAN (dialogue box lower right corner)
Breakfast is up, Sammi!

PANEL FOUR

EXT. FOREST - DAY

A small, stuffed pig lies on the ground.

NARRATIVE BOX
Zuckerman's Pass Cascade Range, Washington State

ALAN (off panel)
Scrambled eggs with cheese! And not the cheap brand like mom buys!
It's super melty!

ALAN (off panel bottom)
Uh, I think you're missing someone.
You dropped...

PANEL FIVE

Medium. Alan, dressed for the outdoors. He holds the stuffed pig.

ALAN
...Fern.

PANEL SIX

Medium. Alan looks at the stuffed pig.

CMAN (dialogue box)
Sometimes there is a place in the soul where hope is kept buried deep and masked...

PANEL SEVEN

Distraught, Alan clutches Fern the stuffed pig.

CMAN (dialogue box)
...a hidden place where savage things grow and dread rustles.

PANEL EIGHT (inset)

ECU. Alan's mouth, he's screaming to the sky.

CMAN (dialogue box)
I knew she was gone forever.

PAGE FIVE

PANEL ONE (inset)

EXT. CITY BLOCK - INTERSECTION

CU of CMan's fangs

CMAN (dialogue box)
I was her father...

MAIN PANEL

CMan grimaces as he pries a Spider-creatures jaw's apart.

CMAN (dialogue box)
Her protector...

PANEL TWO

The Spider-Creature explodes in a burst of gore, innards, and insects.

CMAN (dialogue box)
I failed her and she paid with her life. As did I.

PANEL THREE

The husk of vanquished Spider-creature in BG. CMan stares angrily off-panel.

CMAN
You die next, pig man!

PAGE SIX

EXT. CITY BLOCK - DAY

FULL PAGE

A MAN in a leather bondage-style pig mask hovers above the ground on a 'sky-sled'. This is CRONIN BRAZEL. Cman, with the bodies of several dead foes at his feet, looks up at Cronin. Large spiders with the heads of pigs crawl on nearby buildings.

> CRONIN
> Is that what you believe, Monnnn-ster? Why do you mainnnn-tain loyalty to the architects of your malignannn-t existence?

INSET PANEL ONE:

Medium: Cronin.

> CRONIN
> What was promised you to destroy me and protect their portals?

INSET PANEL TWO:

ECU: Cronin's Eye.

> CRONIN
> That *you* would become a savior?

INSET PANEL THREE:

The cosmos. Black hole. Stars.

> CRONIN (dialogue box)
> A god amongst the weakened masses? He who would lead mankind to salvation through valleys of darkness and the profane?

INSET PANEL FOUR:

ECU: A Gray Alien's eye.

> CRONIN (dialogue box)
> Was the return of your soul the bait they used, Monnn-ster?

INSET PANEL FIVE:

Close: Full face of a classic 'Gray' alien.

> CRONIN (dialogue box)
> ...Or shall I assume it was lost forever, along with all that was precious to you?

PAGE SEVEN

INT. ALIEN LABORATORY - NIGHT
(Bio-mechanical feel to surroundings)

PANEL ONE

CMan POV. Several Gray Aliens hover over him. Behind them, a 'fetus' floats in a glass bubble.

> CMAN (dialogue box)
> By their hand, I entered the flesh. Resurrected. This time, I am changed. Carved not in the image of man, but of Angels. Angels...

PANEL TWO

Tools laid out on a tray for an operation.

>>> CMAN (dialogue box)
>>> ...and torment.

PANEL THREE

CMan deformed face. A work in progress.

>>> CMAN (dialogue box)
>>> I was filled with the roiling winds of time and was sorrowful, because with unmitigated clarity ...

PANEL FOUR

Wider shot of CMan's body on the surgical table.

>>> CMAN (dialogue box)
>>> ...I knew that the futility of God's endeavor was absolute.

PANEL FIVE

A Gray holds a slug-like creature with a pair of forceps.

>>> CMAN (dialogue box)
>>> I *am* the knowledge of the ages. I *am* the design of contrary. I *am* vengeance.

PANEL SIX

Cronin smiles at something off-panel.

>>> CMAN (dialogue box upper left corner)
>>> It's been said, Jesus wept.

>>> CMAN (dialogue box lower right corner)
>>> I will not.

PAGE EIGHT

SIDEBAR

Cronin on sky sled.

PANEL ONE

Medium. Cronin.

>>> CRONIN
>>> Have you connn-sidered your maker may have erased the painnn-ful memories carried from your huma-nnn form?

PANEL TWO

Medium. CMan looking up at Cronin.

CRONIN
Shed your anguish ?

PANEL THREE

Cronin on sky sled looking down at CMan

CRONIN
What kind of father burdens his only son in such a way?

PANEL FOUR

CU. Cman eyes.

CRONIN (dialogue box)
They are using your agonnn-y... to forgive their sinnn-s.

PANEL FIVE

Sign for a roadside restaurant.

VOICE (off panel)
I'm telling you Wilbur, it ain't him.

VOICE #2 (off panel)
Hush, hush sweet Charlotte...

PAGE NINE

PANEL ONE

A bearded Alan Ostman is on his hands and knees. A bully, WILBUR flanked by a woman, CHARLOTTE, has knocked Alan to the ground.

WILBUR
...'isss him. Fer shore...

CHARLOTTE
Yeah, but he got a beard and all.

WILBUR
Fuck his hairy-ass face! I couldn't never forgit a kisser like 'dat. Even wit' his shit disguise!

INSET PANEL ONE

CU of Wilbur.

WILBUR
Trus' me. I seen his pitcher' on the inner'net lotsa' times.

INSET PANEL TWO

Medium of Alan on ground.

ALAN
You didn't happen to be using the "inner'net" at the "liberry", did you?

PANEL THREE

Wilbur preparing to deliver a punch.

WILBUR
Keep crackin' wise, why don'cha? 'Cept it's me, not your kid you up against 'an...

PANEL FOUR

Alan, on ground, reels.

WILBUR (off panel)
...maybe it's *you* they won' be findin' hide nor hair of...

PANEL FIVE

Wilbur sees something off-panel. Charlotte flees.

WILBUR
...this time.

PANEL SIX

Medium. Alan on ground. Gray aliens behind him.

ALAN
Huh?!

PANEL SEVEN

Gray alien.
Untraditional word balloon. Imply telepathic communication.

ALIEN
Ostman.

PANEL EIGHT

Cronin.

CRONIN
I imagine little Sammi...

PAGE TEN

PANEL ONE

CU of zipper mouth.

CRONIN
...must smell almost as bad as you do by now.

PANEL TWO

CMan enraged. He leaps at Cronin.

> CMAN
> You...don't...say...her..

PANEL THREE

Cronin fires a heat ray from his sky sled.

> CMAN
> ...NAME!

> CRONIN
> Down boy!

PANEL FOUR

CMan burned by heat ray. He screams in pain.

> CRONI
> Bad dog!

> CMAN
> Ahhhhhhh!!!

> CRONIN
> EeeeeHaaaaa!!

PAGE ELEVEN

EXT. ROADSIDE DINER - PARKING LOT - NIGHT

PANEL ONE

A Gray Alien obliterates the bully with a heat ray. Charlotte reacts in horror.

> CHARLOTTE
> Wilbur!

PANEL TWO

Charlotte flees. Wilbur is a pile of ash. Alan, on the ground, looks at the Gray Alien.

PANEL THREE

The Gray Alien extends hand its to Alan who shrinks away.

> ALIEN
> Ostman.

PANEL FOUR

Closer on Alan looking at something off-panel.

ALAN
How...

PAGES TWELVE-THIRTEEN

EXT. ROADSIDE DINER - PARKING LOT - MOMENTS LATER

SPLASH PAGE

Two or three Gray Aliens stand next to man who is still on ground. An enormous ALIEN MOTHER SHIP hovers above the tree line.

ALAN
My name...how did you...what do you want?

ALIEN
Our desire is within Ostman. Within. You know. Haven't you always known?

PAGE FOURTEEN

One panel repeated. Snaking around the page. Sammi through the portal.

SAMMI
Daddy? I can't see you

PAGE FIFTEEN

FULL PAGE

Backdrop of the pig mask with six circular panels. Place dialogue boxes where convenient.

CRONIN (dialogue box)
You *do* realize the authors of the abominnn-ation you've become created the very portal your child ennn-tered that day?

CRONIN
(dialogue box)
Not to mentio-nnn the cryptids who guard them.

CRONIN
(dialogue box)
They are well sequestered, your brethren. Once I find and annn-ihilate the remainnn-der, the Hostile dimennn-sion will opennn wide and evil beyond what you could possibly fathom will sup on your world and annn-y others we so desire.

PANEL ONE

Bigfoot.

NARRATIVE BOX
A-nnn ape-like giannn-t that innn-habits the forests of the Pacific Nnn-orthwest.

PANEL TWO

The Loch Ness Monster.

NARRATIVE BOX
An elusive lake monnn-ster The Surgeo-nnn is the onnn-ly onnn-e to
have committed her to film.

PANEL THREE

Long, narrow panel. The pig mask's eyeholes burn brightly. His eyes are a part of the BG Pig
Mask image.

PANEL FOUR

The Jersey Devil.

NARRATIVE BOX
Thirteennn-th child of Mother Leeds. Cursed at birth as a demonnn by
its ow-nnn mother.

PANEL FIVE

Mothman.

NARRATIVE BOX
The red-eyed fiennn-d of West Virginnn-ia.

PANEL SIX

Chupacabra.

NARRATIVE BOX
Unnn-cleannn miscreationnn. Drinnn-ker of blood.

PANEL SEVEN

The Abominable Snowman.

NARRATIVE BOX
The glacier beinnn-g of the Himalayas.

PAGE SIXTEEN

PANEL ONE

Cronin hovers over CMan. A burn on CMan's chest is evident.

CRONIN
How must it feel to be in service of those who spilled the blood of the
onnn-e you held dearest. Oh, monnn-ster...

PANEL TWO

Cronin. Sadistic expression

CRONIN
...you may as well have se-nnn-te-nnnced her to the slab yourself.

PANEL THREE

CMan reacting angrily.

CMAN
You lie!

PANEL FOUR

CMan's Loch Ness arm locked around Cronin's neck

CRONIN
Oh my!

PAGE SEVENTEEN

PANEL ONE

CMan rips Cronin from his sky-sled.

CRONIN
I once knew a woma-nnn, a lovely perso-nnn by annn-yone's stannn-dards.

PANEL TWO

Cman throws Cronin into the side of a building.

CRONIN
How she loved to be punnn-ished!

PANEL THREE

Cronin crashes to ground.

CRONIN
Oooooo...the nnn-oises she would make, let me tell you! Like an annn-imal.

PANEL FOUR

Close on Cronin. Blood seeps from corner of his mouth through zipper.

CRONIN
...and all I got from the old man's side of the family was a receding hairlinnn-e.

CRONIN (separate jagged word balloon)
HAHAHAHAHAHAHAHA!!!

PANEL FIVE

Cronin about to be clobbered by CMan. Lettering to indicate he's using a child's voice.

CRONIN
Daddy? I can't find Fern. Have you seen her?

PANEL SIX

CMan stops mid-attack.

CMAN
Sammi?

EXT. SUBURBAN NEIGHBORHOOD - PORCH - DAY

PANEL ONE

Same view as page one but woman isn't in panel. Sky is a preternatural color.

> DIALOGUE BOX
> The angels taught me one can only know themselves after death, as they did before the womb.

PANEL TWO

Mrs. Hammond's dog in throes of death. Mrs. Hammond has horrified look as a CREATURE bursts from the dogs carcass.

> DIALOGUE BOX
> Lucifer.

PANEL FOUR

Eddie the paperboy on ground in shock, both arms severed. A hostile crouches looking at him, almost in curiosity.

> DIALOGUE BOX
> Beelzebub.

PANEL FIVE

The adulterous couple in bed being swarmed by pig-spiders or other small, vicious creatures.

> DIALOGUE BOX
> Asmodeus.

PANEL SIX

Wide. Almost overhead view of suburban neighborhood. Faint image of Pig Mask in sky. Bodies float in an ocean of blood.

> DIALOGUE BOX (upper left corner)
> Constructs of man's obsession with understanding his world.

> DIALOGUE BOX (lower right corner)
> Arrogance and fear cloaked in earnest pursuit of glimpsing reason beyond mortality realizing its boundary.

PAGE NINETEEN

EXT. CITY BLOCK - DAY

PANEL ONE

Cronin lays at Cman's feet.

> CRONIN
> Say it ai-nnn't so! Is the funnn over already?

PANEL TWO

CMan falls to his knees next to Cronin.

> CMAN
> Sammi...How could you know? Unless...

PANEL THREE

CMan POV looking at Cronin.

> CRONIN
> Unnn-less...Yes, look at me monnn-ster!
> Unnn-less...Say it!

PANEL FOUR

Closer. The eye holes of Cronin's pig mask glow slightly.

> CRONIN
> You ca-nnnn't believe it to be true?
> Cannn you?

PAGE TWENTY

PANEL ONE

The pig mask's eyes glow brightly. Otherworldly.

> CRONIN
> Wherever light seeks refuge...

PANEL TWO

Beams of light emit from The pig mask's snout.

> CRONIN
> ...darkness shall surely pursue.

PANEL THREE

CU. Long Panel. Fingers pulling the mouth zipper open.

PANEL FOUR

Full shot of Cronin with his arms extended, Christ-like. Light bursts from the pig mask's eyes, nose, and mouth.

> CRONIN
> Fools and dreamers profess that faith defeats the eclipse of their
> humannn-ity...

PAGE TWENTY-ONE

PANEL ONE

Pig Mask in silhouette with an aura of bright light surrounding him. Cman on ground, his eyes burning from the light.

> CRONIN
> ...but *know* the cimmeriannn onnne will always, ALWAYS impregnnn-ate the hollows of its quarry!

PANEL TWO

Windows in surrounding buildings blowing out into the street. Glass flying. Cronin's features are undefined, he's made of light.

> CRONIN
> I AM HE WHO BRINGS THE LIGHT, THE SHINING ONE. OPPOSE ME AND SUFFER A THOUSAND LIFETIMES IN THE PIT OF WAILING SOULS!

PANEL THREE

Cronin (still undefined, made of light) reaches for CMan who for the first time, appears terrified.

> CRONIN
> Take my hand, monnn-ster.

PANEL FOUR

Cronin takes CMan by the hand.

> CRONIN
> TAKE IT!

PAGE TWENTY-TWO

Full page. Cronin and CMan enter an inter-dimensional portal.

> CRONIN
> ...your little girl waits.

To be continued...

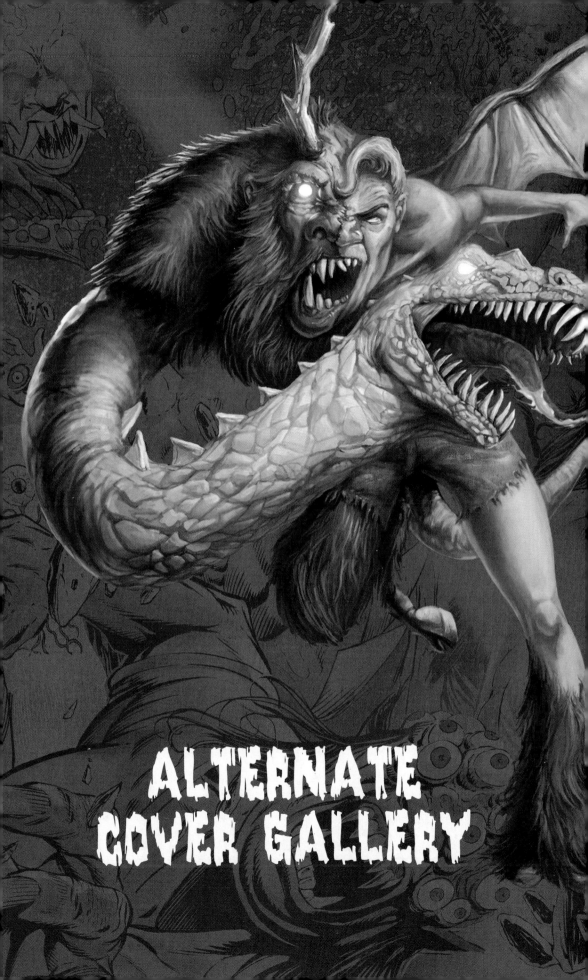

ALTERNATE
COVER GALLERY

CRYPTOZOICMAN

DYNAMITE

BRYAN JOHNSON • WALTER FLANAGAN

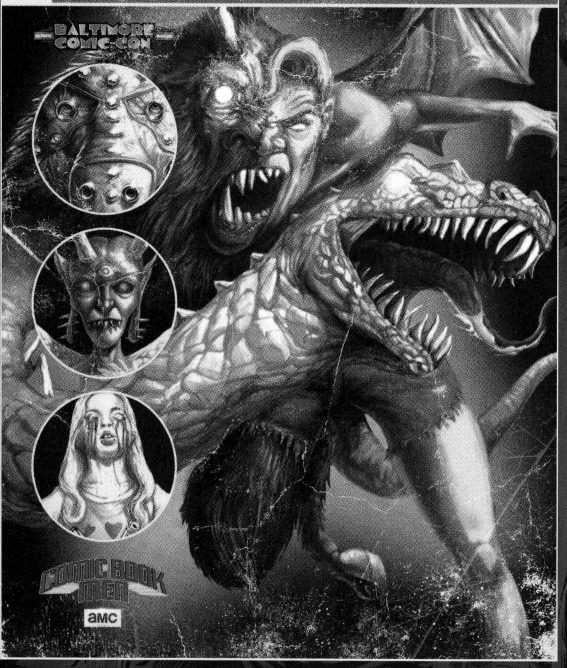

ISSUE #1 BALTIMORE COMICON EXCLUSIVE COVER
art by WALTER FLANAGAN colors by WAYNE JANSEN

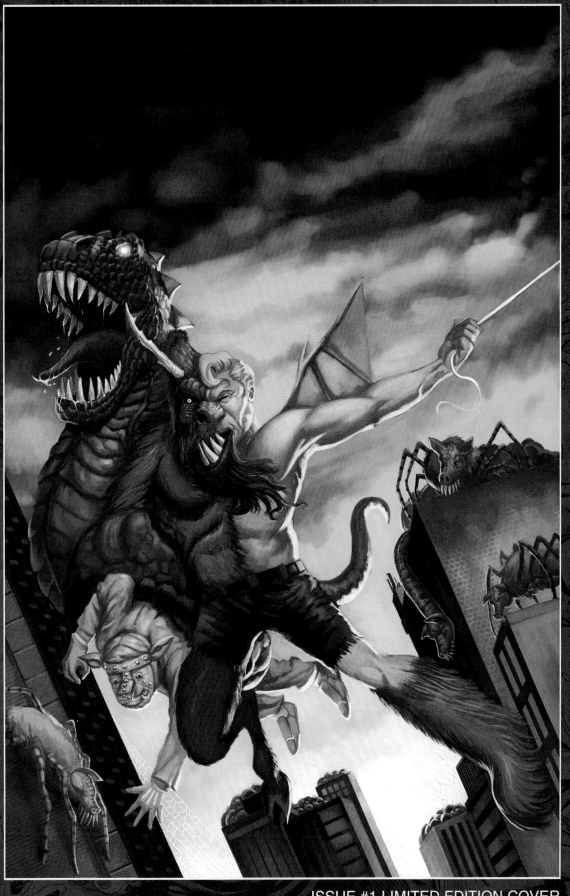

ISSUE #1 LIMITED EDITION COVER
art by **WALTER FLANAGAN** colors by **WAYNE JANSEN**

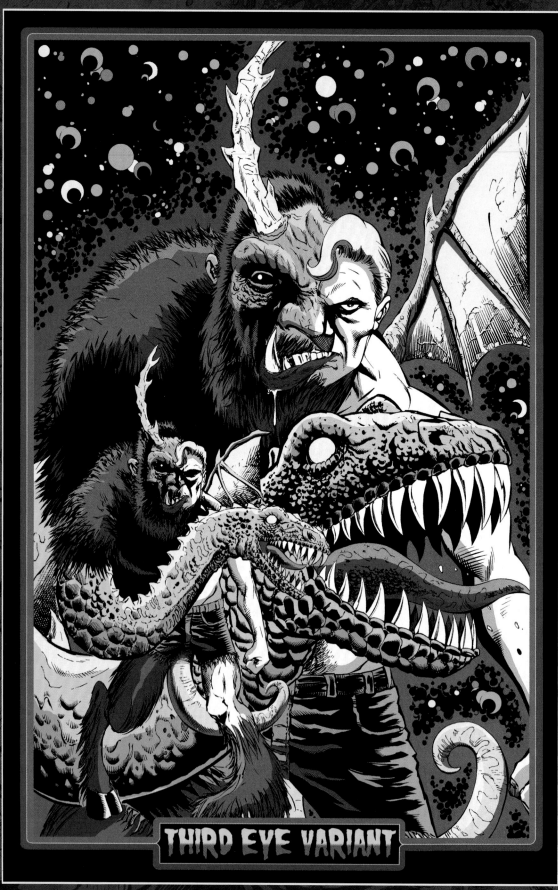

THIRD EYE VARIANT

ISSUE #1 JETPACK COMICS EXCLUSIVE COVER
art by **WALTER FLANAGAN** colors by **WAYNE JANSEN**

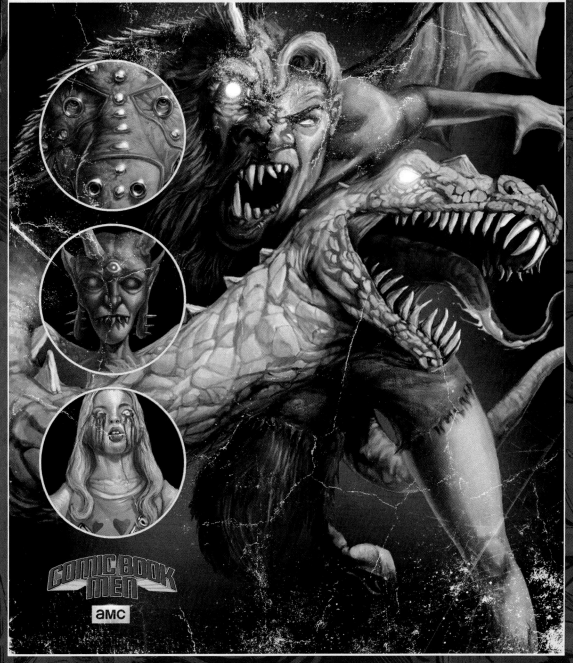

AS SEEN ON THE amc SERIES COMIC BOOK MEN!

#1

DYNAMITE

CRYPTOZOICMAN

BRYAN JOHNSON • WALTER FLANAGAN

ISSUE #1 SECOND PRINT COVER
art by **WALTER FLANAGAN** colors by **WAYNE JANSEN**

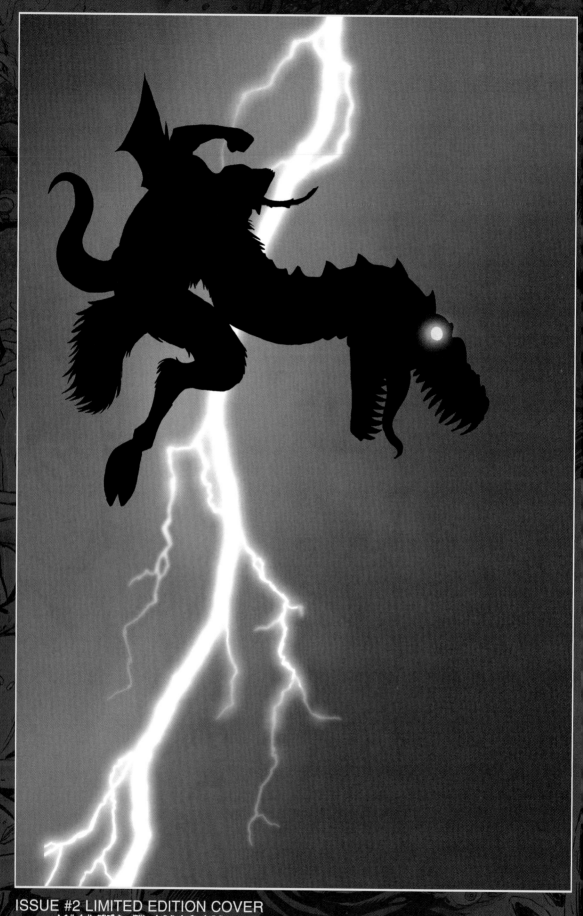

ISSUE #2 LIMITED EDITION COVER
art by **WALTER FLANAGAN** colors by **WAYNE JANSEN**

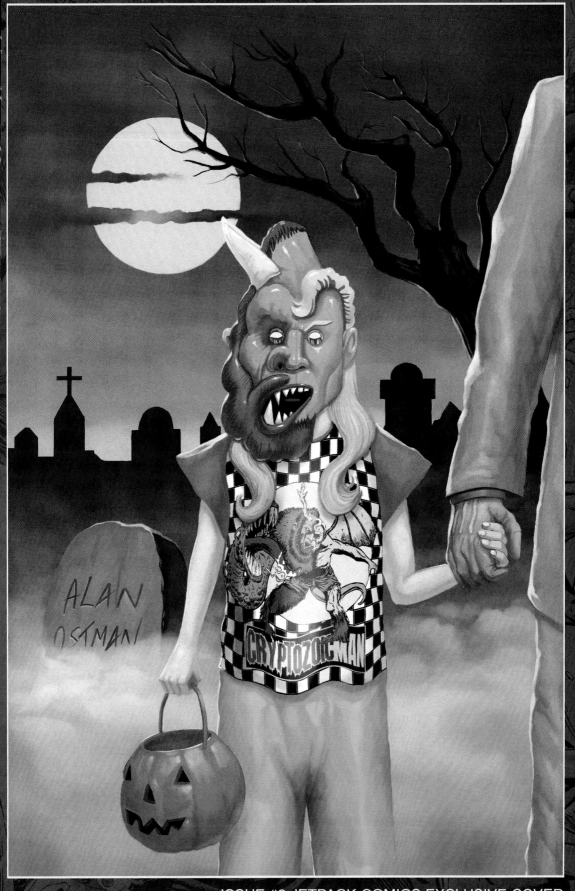

ISSUE #2 JETPACK COMICS EXCLUSIVE COVER
art by **WALTER FLANAGAN** colors by **WAYNE JANSEN**

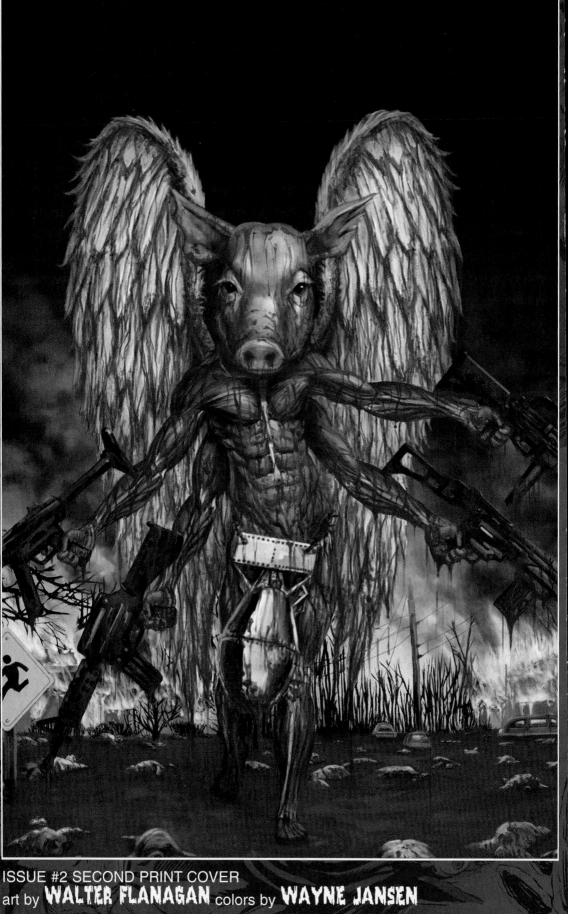

ISSUE #2 SECOND PRINT COVER
art by **WALTER FLANAGAN** colors by **WAYNE JANSEN**

MIGHTIEST MONSTER IN ALL CREATION!

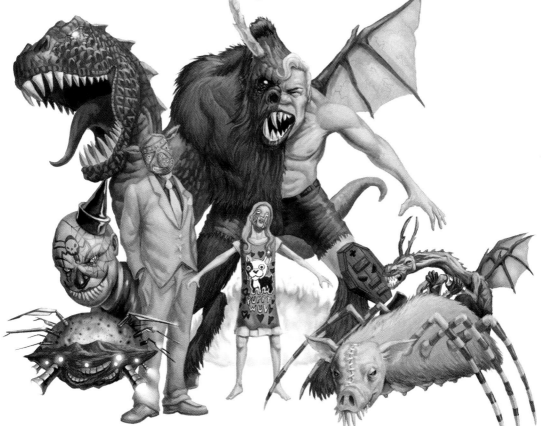

Cryptozoic Man

CRYPTOZOIC MAN BRYAN JOHNSON · WALT FLANAGAN · CHRIS IVY · WAYNE JANSEN

ISSUE #3 LIMTIED EDITION COVER
art by **WALTER FLANAGAN** colors by **WAYNE JANSEN**

DYNAMITE CRYPTOZOIC MAN

JETPACK COMICS EXCLUSIVE 3

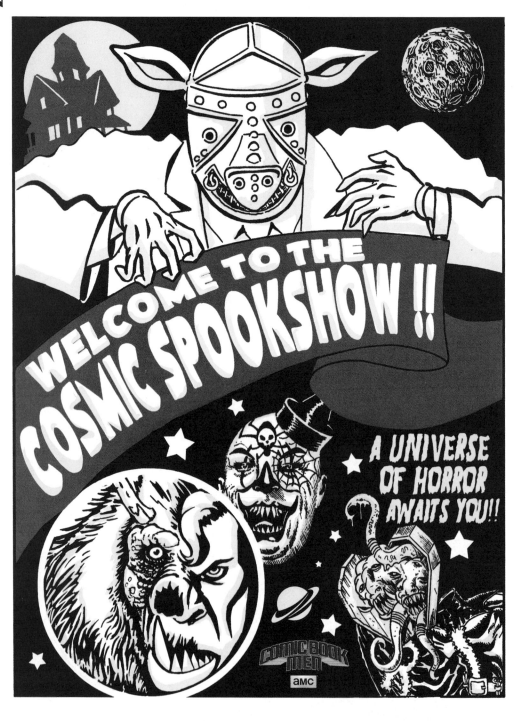

WELCOME TO THE COSMIC SPOOKSHOW !!

A UNIVERSE OF HORROR AWAITS YOU!!

COMIC BOOK MEN amc

ISSUE #3 JETPACK COMICS EXCLUSIVE COVER
art by **WALTER FLANAGAN** colors by **WAYNE JANSEN**

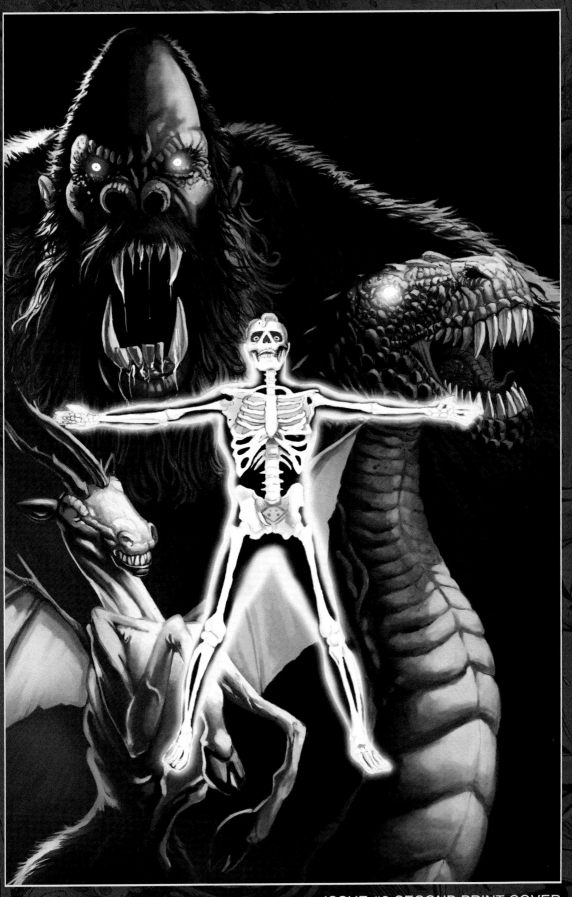

ISSUE #3 SECOND PRINT COVER
art by **WALTER FLANAGAN** colors by **WAYNE JANSEN**

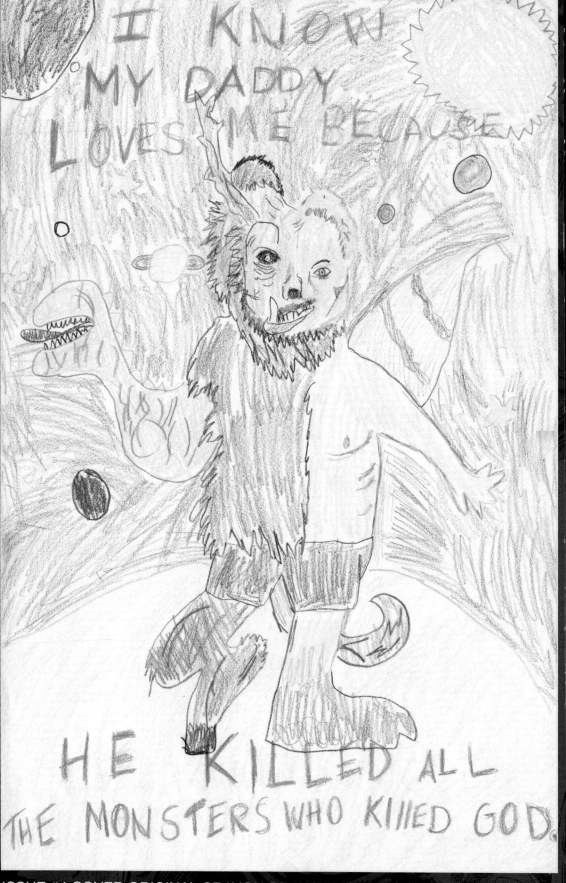

ISSUE #4 COVER ORIGINAL CRAYON DRAWING
art by **ALICIA FLANAGAN**

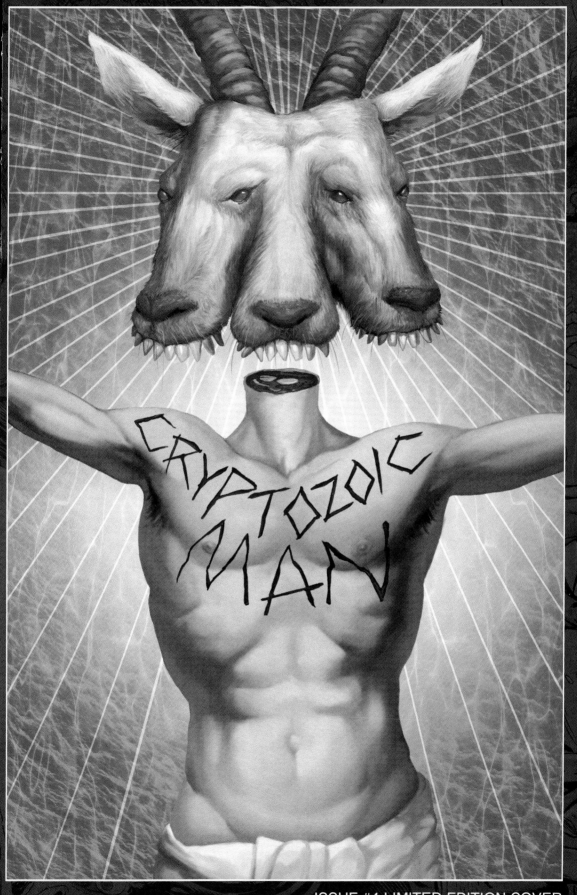

ISSUE #4 LIMITED EDITION COVER
art by **WALTER FLANAGAN** colors by **WAYNE JANSEN**

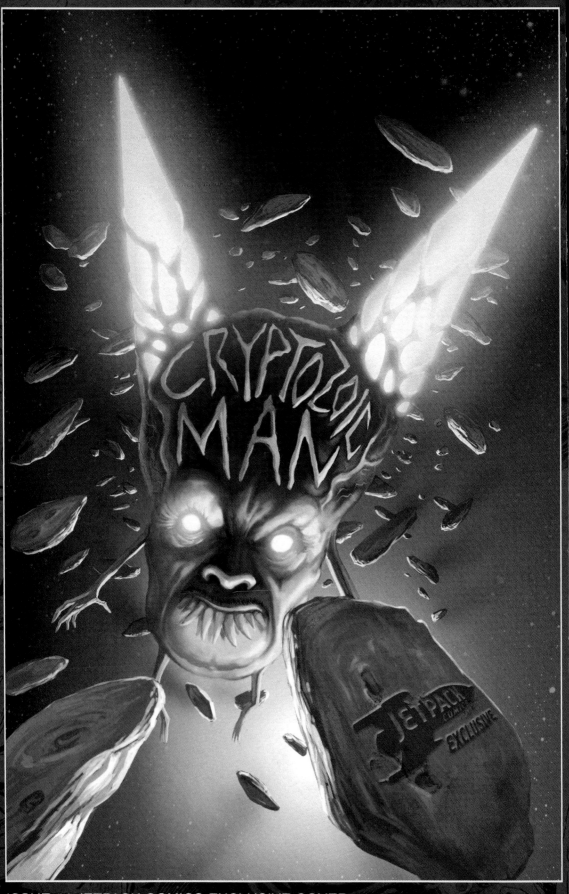

ISSUE #4 JETPACK COMICS EXCLUSIVE COVER
art by **WALTER FLANAGAN** colors by **WAYNE JANSEN**

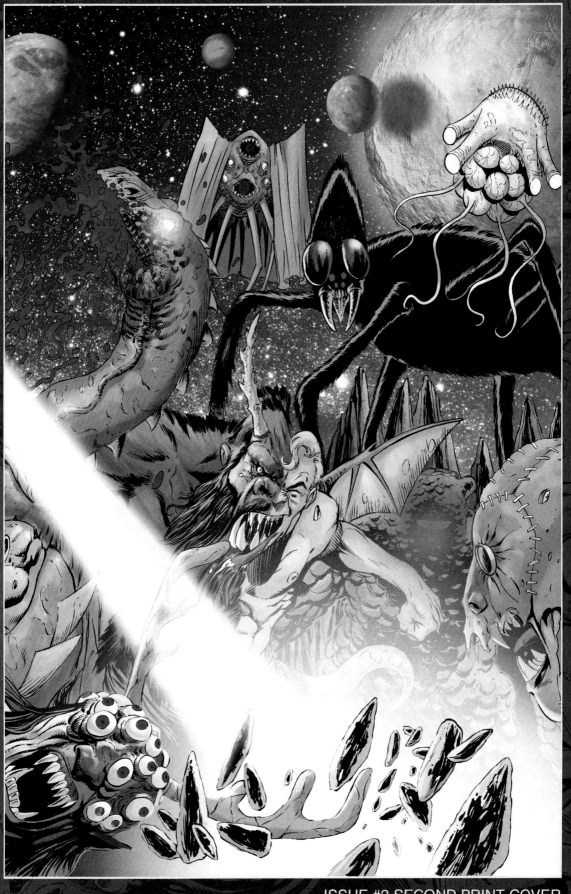

ISSUE #2 SECOND PRINT COVER
art by **WALTER FLANAGAN** colors by **WAYNE JANSEN**